What People Are Saying

Our whole family has enjoyed The Messengers series. . . . These characters are doing what I most desire for my children: they treasure the Word. These Messengers share the Word, they call upon it in trouble, they encourage one another with the Word, and they desire to share it. All of this wrapped into an edgy, high-adventure novel that captures readers from the first chapter! It should be required reading for parents of our generation.

Jennifer Janssen, homeschooling mom of fifth and sixth graders

Lisa Clark's contemplative, insightful, and edifying narrative matures right alongside Simon in the third installment of The Messengers series. No worldly drivel marks the page in this story of persecution, only thoughtful expressions of the endurance, character, and hope produced in the life of the Christian through suffering. This fictional series is a catechetical gift to our children, one that points toward God's Word, His Church, and the eternal hope that will not put the baptized to shame.

Katie Schuermann, author of the Anthems of Zion series

A strong finish to a remarkable series. Lisa Clark has gifted us all with a poignant and beautiful story. The setting is hauntingly realistic and believable in these gray and latter days of life under the cross. The characters are compelling and endearing, flawed and imperfect, as are we all, yet struggling to live by faith and in love for one another. . . . What I have loved and appreciated most about the entire series is the way it weaves the confession and practice of the faith so naturally into the warp and woof of the story. . . . It is comforting encouragement, indeed, for such times as these.

Pastor Rick Stuckwisch, Emmaus Lutheran Church,
South Bend, Indiana

In *Revealed*, Simon grows and matures as a young Christian man as he faces the reality of Satan's many means of attacking, both physical and spiritual. Simon learns how to die, but also how to live, echoing the baptismal life we all share. Lisa's ability to tackle tough subjects seamlessly within the narrative, along with the use of Scripture and hymnody, leaves the reader with the hope that only God in Christ can give. My ten-year-old can't wait for this installment, and this is exactly the kind of reading material I hope to give him.

Elizabeth Ahlman, author of Demystifying the Proverbs 31 Woman
and Ruth: More Than a Love Story

Once again, Lisa Clark captures the attention of the reader with our boy Simon's struggle to understand his past and how it intertwines with the events happening in the present. High appreciation to the author for using the dystopian genre to paint a picture of the urgency to spread the Gospel message to a dying world. . . . One could almost put themselves in the catacombs beneath New Morgan and sense the drive that Simon and his friends have for the Message.

Elizabeth Decker, LCMS teacher

New Morgan has revoked Simon Clay's citizenship, but it cannot revoke his true citizenship, which comes from heaven. Though the Messengers are always in danger of the oppressive government, Simon is learning that the most oppressive dangers are those of doubt, despair, and distrust. Armed with the Word of God and supported by the small communion of saints that it sustains, Simon is prepared to risk it all for the Message worth dying for. *Revealed* is a fast-paced and fitting conclusion to this trilogy.

Timothy Koch, pastor at Concordia and Immanuel Lutheran
churches, reviewer at TheBeggarsBlog.com

Clark weaves the page-turning lore of dystopian literature with the never-changing truth of Scripture. My students were hooked from the first chapter. Simon is a relatable character to today's young adult. He wrestles with many conflicts as his readers are beginning to ask deeper questions about their faith. In this way, people of all ages can not only value *Revealed* as an exciting work of fiction but also as a story that points to Jesus.

Mrs. Faith Wiechers, middle school language arts teacher,
St. Paul Lutheran School, Napoleon, Ohio

Revealed continues to create meaningful discussion for youth and young adults around big questions, while continuing to bring us characters and a storyline that is both intriguing and comforting. In this installment, Clark does not disappoint, compelling readers to sort through questions of good and evil and to identify who the real enemies in our lives are, the importance and pricelessness of genuine community and connection, and the treasure of the Word that we so often take for granted.

Deaconess Heidi Goehmann, I Love My Shepherd Ministries and
author of Altogether Beautiful

In The Messengers series, Lisa M. Clark weaves a compelling tale of faith and courage based on the Word. It is so compelling, so personal, that I began this third book with a certain amount of apprehension. What would happen to Simon and the Messengers in these pages? How will they deal with loss and grief? betrayal? relationships? new challenges? old wounds? Read to find the answers, and don't be surprised if this story becomes woven into your own.

Eden Keefe, LWML Vice-President of Christian Life 2013–2017,
Visual Faith Coach, www.visualfaithmin.org

Filled with excitement, suspense, and plenty of the logos, *Revealed* is a must-read for fans of the first two books in the trilogy. It is a powerful reminder of who we can turn to when it seems as though we are all alone. Simon's and the other Messengers' responses to challenges . . . are constant reminders of God's everlasting faithfulness and love. I could hardly bring myself to put it down!

Faith Musgrave, teen and avid reader

I was both saddened and uplifted when I reached the end of *Revealed*. The entire series was so engaging, and now I'll miss the characters. I can't imagine a more fitting final installment. . . . Clark not only asked the hard questions, but leaned into them, grabbed hold of them, and wrestled with them. And always with Scripture at the core of it all. I definitely recommend this book, and the entire series, for anyone looking for good YA dystopian fiction!

Sarah Baughman, author of forthcoming novel A Flame in the Dark

In *Revealed*, Simon works through the pain of personal loss to find peace and then spurs his friends on to hold even firmer to their hope in Christ. His steady transformation into a passionate man of God is a satisfying progression! The author expertly intersects the lives of the apostles with those of Simon, Charity, and others, thus beautifully showing the continuity of the Church over time. *Revealed* is a refreshing reminder that nothing can suppress the light of Jesus Christ. It will continue to shine, age after age, present in the Word and alive in the hearts of His Bride, the Church.

Heather Kaufman, author of The Story People and Loving Isaac

An outstanding read and exciting conclusion to The Messengers trilogy! Clark delivers, once again, as she launches her readers into a dystopian world not unlike our own. Youth and adults alike are certain to find encouragement in the faith as they join young Simon and the underground Church on the mission to spread God's Word. Persecution, martyrdom, war: nothing can stop the λόγος from getting out. It is, after all, the message worth dying (and living) for!

Rev. Tyrel Bramwell, pastor and author of The Gift and the Defender

The Messengers series by Lisa Clark is both captivating and theologically sound. . . . *Revealed* continues to push and challenge Simon, and it will continue to push and challenge the reader to keep sharing the truth.

Stephanie Lebeau, Director of Parish Ed., Ramona Lutheran Church

Prologue

Mrs. Louise Baden-Druck stared at the piece of Maximalus set before her on the table.

"This. Is. Unforgivable!" she shouted.

The three figures on the other side of the table cringed.

She stood and wielded the scrap of metal.

"Our family reputation is at stake. Our government is at stake. How is it that we cannot silence one insignificant boy?!"

She walked toward them.

"Let me tell you one thing, Roderick. And listen to me closely. One of you will survive another year. You or Simon. It's up to you to decide who that's going to be."

■ ■ ■

Other Books in The Messengers Series

Discovered

Concealed

The Messengers

REVEALED

Lisa M. Clark

CONCORDIA PUBLISHING HOUSE • SAINT LOUIS

This book is written in thankfulness to God for all the Zekes,
Ellas, and Mrs. Meyers throughout the ages.

Concordia
Publishing House

Copyright © 2018 Concordia Publishing House
3558 S. Jefferson Avenue, St. Louis, MO 63118-3968
1-800-325-3040 · www.cph.org

Written by Lisa M. Clark

Scripture quotations are from the ESV® Bible (The Holy Bible, English Standard Version®),
copyright © 2001 by Crossway, a publishing ministry of Good News Publishers. Used by
permission. All rights reserved.

Scripture paraphrases are adapted from Scripture quotations are from the ESV® Bible (The
Holy Bible, English Standard Version®), copyright © 2001 by Crossway, a publishing ministry
of Good News Publishers. Used by permission. All rights reserved.

Hymn quotations are public domain and from *Lutheran Service Book*, copyright © 2006
Concordia Publishing House. All rights reserved.

Hymn quotation in chapter 25 is from "When I Behold Jesus Christ" by Almaz Belhu, copyright © 1970 Ethiopian Evangelical Church Mekane Yesus. Used by permission.

Library of Congress Cataloging-in-Publication Data

Names: Clark, Lisa M., author.
Title: The Messengers : revealed / Lisa M. Clark.
Description: St. Louis : Concordia Publishing House, 2018. | Summary: Simon
    and the Messengers begin to discover how big their mission truly is as
    they work harder than ever to share the truth with the world, despite
    having faced great loss and pain.
Identifiers: LCCN 2017048957 (print) | LCCN 2018012584 (ebook) | ISBN
    9780758659620 | ISBN 9780758659613
Subjects: | CYAC: Despotism--Fiction. | Religion--Fiction. | Secret
    societies--Fiction. | Fathers and sons--Fiction. | Insurgency--Fiction. |
    Science fiction.
Classification: LCC PZ7.1.C575 (ebook) | LCC PZ7.1.C575 Mev 2018 (print) |
    DDC [Fic]--dc23

LC record available at https://lccn.loc.gov/2017048957

1   2   3   4   5   6   7   8   9   10   27   26   25   24   23   22   21   20   19   18

Chapter One

Why, oh why, must I always do everything with my brother? We work together. We eat together. And now, we travel the world together. Some men may be fine spending day in and day out with family, but they clearly do not know this thunder-head of a brother I have! Always putting himself first—I cannot bear the way he pushes his way nonstop. You would think that our Teacher would notice what a pain he can be. You would think I could find some time to be away from him. But no, even when Jesus pulls me aside for a lesson or time away, He invites my brother along too. I cannot take it any longer! I tell you the truth; as soon as I can find the occasion, I'm going to get away from him and do things my way for a change.

■ ■ ■

—*Right about now, not far away*—

"Simon . . . Simooooooooooon . . ."

Under his quilt, Simon heard the low moan come from outside his bedroom door.

"It's time, Simoooooon."

The creak of his door and the floorboards declared that the intruder was closing in.

"The Darkness, Siiiiimon. It's coming for yoooooooooooooooou!"

The warning voice rose to a shrill shriek, and Simon's shout rose to meet it as icy cold water splashed through the quilt and onto his head and torso.

Simon leaped up, tossing the soaked blanket aside and standing on his bed to face his attacker.

The culprit, however, was already subdued, curled into a circle on the floor, failing miserably at warding off the hysterical laughter that shook his frame.

"Jack Lane!" Simon spluttered. "I—you—why do I even put up with you?!"

Simon hurled his pillow and blanket onto the unapologetic teenager, who made no attempt to get up or compose himself.

Simon dropped down clumsily to sit on his mattress, assessing the situation as best as anyone could after such a rude awakening. The close quarters of his bedroom were still new to him, as were the brick walls and thin mattress. It was nothing like the room he had known all his life. A pang of sadness grabbed his chest, and Simon didn't push it away. Still, there were familiar things: wooden furniture his dad had crafted, a picture of his family from years ago, and a watch that had become a part of him even in the short time he had owned it. There were new things too—new things that provided comfort rather than a sense of loss: a mural on his ceiling, a painted message on his door, and the handmade quilt Mrs. Meyer had given him. The one that currently half covered Jack with condemnation and water.

"What are you doing here? You have a home, don't you?"

Simon didn't mean for the comment to come out as an accusation, but fatigue and irritation laced his words in a way that Simon immediately regretted. He was learning that formerly innocent phrases could take on new meaning. Jokes that had once been good-natured could sour. Jack had a home, and Simon was constantly reminded that he did not.

"Hey, bright eyes," Jack tossed back, graciously ignoring the jab, "look at the time."

Simon reached for his watch on the top of a bookshelf and tried to make sense of what he saw. It was noon already. Simon rubbed his forehead and remembered the date: Saturday, July 30. Census Day.

"How did you get here during the day anyway?" Simon knew that crowds in Grand Station grew during the weekends, but most Messengers only dared to visit after dark. There were some who found ways to come during daylight hours, but most Messengers considered it too risky.

"I have my ways." Jack shrugged and sat up. "Paid a visit to good ol' Mrs. Meyer. Besides," he added, tossing the quilt aside with dramatic flair, "Ella needs me."

Simon grabbed the quilt and draped it on a wooden chair, allowing it to dry. So Jack had used Mrs. Meyer's tunnel to Grand Station, the City, to impress one of the newest Messengers.

"If you say so." Simon shrugged. "But why are you up here?"

Jack jumped to his feet and dusted himself off. "Someone had to check to see if you were alive." With a wave, Jack was gone.

After a suitable shower, Simon found his assailant faithfully offering his services to a damsel in distress.

"So this is the tool you need then?"

"No."

"How 'bout this one?"

"Nope."

"This one?" At that point, Jack hopped onto a counter after shoving bolts, gears, and a variety of small gadgets aside. With hands stretched wide in invitation, he clearly suggested himself as the cure-all solution.

"No! Honestly, Jack! Can't you find something better to do?" Ella pulled back her safety goggles in exasperation and faced her self-proclaimed hero. Her light hair was tied into a tight knot, but thin wisps escaped any form of entrapment and waved wildly around her face.

"Honestly, Ella? I can't." Jack's grin grew to preposterous levels. All Ella could do was toss a greasy towel at him and turn back to her work.

Simon had witnessed the exchange through the entryway, and now he descended the few stairs into the room they called Spence's cellar to get a better look at the effort at hand.

Ella finally noticed his presence and offered a hearty wave.

"Hey, Simon!" She pulled her goggles back on and crawled under a scant frame that looked just big enough to seat two people.

"What's new?" Simon stood near the counter that separated himself from the workspace and rested his elbows a few feet from Jack's . . . feet.

"Ella's more of a New Morganian than ever," Jack proclaimed. Simon wasn't sure if this was a passive attack or a strange compliment.

Ella finished tightening a few bolts on the machine and stood up. Reaching into her back pocket, she provided explanation.

"Census Day, of course! With my birthday earlier this month, my new card for the year shows my Provisional Adult Status. Did you get yours?"

Once again, an innocent question inflicted silent barbs into Simon, as the sting of his altered reality did its damage.

"I didn't go."

Ella stared for a moment, uncomprehending.

"You didn't go? Simon, all citizens have to go. Today is Census Day! You can't just—wait. It's only noon, right? You have two hours before City Hall closes, and it's just out the North Gate—"

"Ella! I'm not going. I can't go."

Ella shook her head, her pale eyes showing alarm through the large goggles.

"Ella. If I go, they'll arrest me. I can't have any resident status anymore—much less Provisional Adult Status. Who cares how old I am? If my grandmother has her way, I won't be getting any older."

The full weight of his reality hit Ella at once. She dropped to the concrete floor and sat with her legs crossed; a socket wrench escaped her fingers and clanged dully in an anticlimactic protest.

"It isn't fair," she said absently.

"Nope." Simon didn't know what more to say. Jack, who had righted himself to a seated position on the counter during the back-and-forth, leaned forward and rested his forearms on his knees.

"This world is a mess," Ella uttered with quiet solemnity.

"Yep."

In dissonant affirmation, a crash came from behind the back wall of the cellar. All three rushed to an open doorway that led to a wide ramp and, eventually, a hidden passageway. Spence had one arm full of random Bot parts, mechanical odds and ends, and tools. His other arm worked to gather the pieces he had just dropped.

"Gotta create a dramatic entrance, eh, Spence?" Jack's greeting was no surprise to his friends, but Spence responded with only an unimpressed sneer.

Jack bent down to pick up a few stray pieces, but he was interrupted by a reprimand: "Just leave it, Jack. I don't need your help."

Simon caught Ella's eye before she stooped to help her mechanically minded companion. Something wasn't quite right. After all the newfound treasures were stored in appropriate—albeit cluttered—compartments, Jack cleared his throat. The brief hesitation betrayed that he felt slightly less confident than usual.

"Well, Ella, your big day isn't over yet, is it?" Jack inquired.

"The best is yet to come!" Ella's face lit up as she bounced around the workroom in celebration.

"Just remember, Ella," Spence muttered into a box of wire coils, "you're about to renounce the devil and all his ways. I'd be careful if I were you."

Simon didn't know what was going on with Spence, but Jack didn't seem too surprised. His grin was nowhere to be seen, and Jack's shoulders fell with an invisible weight. The next few moments were strange as Jack exited the cellar without much excuse or farewell. Simon shrugged at Ella and followed after.

Jack maneuvered the hallway with speed, weaving around other Messengers who were passing in and out of the main marketplace. Simon instantly noticed the absence of his friend's loud salutations or hearty waves that typically added to the hum of the City. Jack ducked left into the large space filled with booths of all shapes and sizes, and Simon, in an attempt to keep up, almost ran into a middle-aged man carrying a large crate.

Simon mumbled an apology and continued to trail Jack until he stopped under a tent in the middle of the marketplace. The man holding post nodded quietly as Jack approached and headed straight toward a large book.

"Hi, Sol," Simon offered to the man seated on a folding chair near a tent pole. The kindly gentleman waved and faced forward. Evidently, Sol picked up on Jack's need for little interference and didn't strike up a conversation.

"Where is it?" Jack called.

"What's that?" Simon turned and stepped closer to his friend, who was flipping through the pages of an album, hunting for something within the collection of writings in front of him.

"Where's that part about Judas?"

"Which part do you mean? He was in several places, you know."

Jack shot a look of annoyance at Simon as his only comeback and flipped more pages.

"Hey, easy with that," Simon warned. He knew these pages were only copies of the Word, duplicates of texts that were kept safely in Archives throughout the city of Westbend, but any collection of the Scriptures was precious. They were the Message worth dying for, as Simon was keenly aware.

Jack closed the book and turned toward Simon. His eyes burned with anger and hurt, and Simon couldn't make sense of the expression—he'd never seen it on Jack before.

"When Judas dies. What do people say about him? What do they do? Are the disciples all pointing fingers at each other or are they, you know, talking more about Jesus and the end of the world as they knew it? Did they just shrug their shoulders and move on, or did they tear each other apart?"

Simon could only stare back. He had no idea where all of this was coming from, and he definitely had no idea what to say.

Jack shook his head and started to walk back into the aisle. Two steps away from the tent, Jack stopped as a young woman holding a baby called out to him.

"You, there. Jack, is it? You were friends with that Micah character, weren't you? You could tell me, couldn't you? I've heard it said that he—"

But that was all she could toss his way before Jack vanished in the crowd.

Chapter Two

Simon didn't see Jack for hours, but he knew there would be one event Jack wouldn't miss. As midnight approached, Simon walked back through the marketplace to a room that was quickly becoming a gallery showcasing the work of his favorite artist.

"The masterpieces of Charity Evans!" Simon had walked into the room with exaggerated grandeur, but his right arm dangled awkwardly aloft as he stopped in the middle of the room. He wasn't good at grandeur.

A small form crouched farther down the wall, holding a paintbrush to a massive apostle's right foot. She mumbled a reply, but Simon didn't catch it.

"What did you say?" Simon asked, walking toward the tenth painted man and his creator.

"I said," Charity said louder but with the same tone, "that if I were doing this for myself, I'd have quit long ago." She rolled back from her careful squatting position and spread herself out on the floor—face toward the ceiling, arms splayed out in dramatized exhaustion. "Art is hard."

But essential, Simon mused. He knew that sharing his thoughts would sound trivial, but he could remember the first time he had left the world of gray superficiality above and entered this subterranean world of beauty and light.

"Well, I like art," Simon asserted, going for a ridiculously light approach. "And artists." With that, he sat himself near Charity's head and looked up at her newest work. Still focused on the wall, he brushed Charity's tousled hair back to her careful part. He was doing his best to seem absentminded about it all.

"Census Day was today."

Charity's head nodded under his hand.

"I'm officially not official."

"Welcome to the club." Charity's voice wasn't as flippant as her words. There were tones of sadness and empathy there. Simon swallowed hard.

"I don't know if I can do this, Charity." Simon appreciated the growing closeness the two shared, and the growing willingness to be honest with each other. Still, his voice couldn't raise much above a whisper.

Charity pulled herself up to sit next to him. Simon glanced toward her and saw her green eyes training on the work before them.

"I didn't think I could either," she admitted softly. "Others have helped. You helped." After a pause, she took his right hand in her left. "I'll try to help you."

Three footsteps echoed, and Simon and Charity turned to see Jack near the large entrance where Simon had come in. His hands were in his pockets, and he slowly rotated, as if he were casually visiting the gallery surrounding them.

"Hey, Jack," Simon called. He was relieved to see his friend after such a strange exchange in the marketplace, but he didn't want to appear concerned.

Jack turned halfway toward them and offered a small, quick wave. Simon stood, brushed himself off, and walked to Jack.

"Is it time?" Simon pressed. "You'll want a good seat."

Jack's smile was pained. Simon hated it. He wanted to reverse time to that obnoxiously goofy smile Jack flashed on the day they had first met. Simon wanted to reverse time often.

"Come on, boys," Charity inserted, coming from behind Simon and leading them into the marketplace.

The three walked into one of Simon's favorite spots of the City; he could never help touching the mosaic that surrounded them as they made their way down the hall. This time, he placed his hand on the vivid red and orange field, close to the cross.

"Have you ever made mosaics?" Simon asked Charity, looking up under the looming cross.

"No," Charity answered. "Maybe someday. I wish I could have learned from whoever made this one."

"Maybe it was a team effort," Jack commented.

Simon was encouraged that Jack spoke, but discouraged that it was not some sort of quip. *What is wrong with me? I actually want Jack to act dumb?* Simon forced himself to nod and turned back to head down the hallway.

Charity made it to the end of the hallway first and pushed open the heavy door to reveal the octagonal mahogany room. The lamps were dim, and the room was empty. Jack moved briskly to the far wall, sliding the concealed door aside. The stone room beyond was filled with light and laughter; the three eagerly joined the others.

Ella Maxon's bright laugh rang high above the rest, and the friends saw her standing in front of all the pews. Her face radiated joy as she ran to embrace all three in a group hug. Simon instinctively knew that this would have been an opportune time for Jack to tease Ella, but Jack wasn't even reacting to the arms around him. His focus was behind Simon, and Simon craned his neck to meet Spence's blank stare.

The banter hushed, and everyone found a place to sit. Ella sat between her parents in the front pew on the left. Spence sat farther down the pew, alone. Simon, Jack, and Charity scooted in behind the Maxons. Charity gave Ella's shoulder an encouraging squeeze. A sound to Simon's left and a hearty slap on the back announced that Ben had arrived and joined the group. Simon turned to greet him and saw Dr. Pharen slowly make his way to Ben's side. It suddenly occurred to Simon how dramatically Ben's dad had aged in the past few months.

Simon smiled as he watched Ella in front of him struggle to keep from bouncing in her place. He knew she'd been waiting for this day. Her parents took turns glancing at her, their faces looking both excited and wistful. Simon could only imagine the emotions this family must be feeling. He was proud of Ella, who made every effort to model forgiveness to her parents; they no doubt felt remorse that it was *she* who brought *them* back to the Word.

Elder Cyril's voice broke through Simon's thoughts with a reading from Scripture. "'Go therefore and make disciples of all nations, baptizing them in the name of the Father and of the Son and of the Holy Spirit.' Matthew, chapter twenty-eight."

Elder Johann read next. "'Whoever believes and is baptized will be saved.' Mark, chapter sixteen."

Elder Zeke finished with a grin that stretched his face wide. "'Baptism now saves you.' First Peter, chapter three."

Ella rose and joined the pastors at a column that came up to her elbow. Made of stone, the wide column had eight corners, with a carving on each side. From his perspective, Simon could see one image: a rainbow spanned over a huge boat. Simon couldn't see from his angle, but he knew the column, the font, was filled with water.

Elder Cyril began asking Ella questions that sounded similar to the questions Zeke had asked him merely four months ago.

"Ella, do you renounce the devil?"

Simon smirked as he remembered his own emphatic affirmation. He certainly had seen glimpses of the devil's work then. Simon frowned. *Even more so now.*

"Do you renounce all his works?"

Ella's answers were clear and strong, and Simon couldn't help beaming. That is, until he looked to his right and saw Jack's reddened face cast downward. Simon looked up and to his left to see Spence looking back in Jack's direction with narrowed eyes and pursed lips. Simon's stomach dropped. He recognized that look. But he'd never seen it on Spence's face before. He had seen it on Micah's.

Oh, Micah. Sadness washed over Simon for the friend he had lost over . . . what? Suspicion? Jealousy? No, that wasn't quite it. Simon hated to remember it, but he clung to a vivid image at this moment: Micah's face mixed with pain, regret, sorrow, and finally relief. Then nothing.

"Ella," Zeke called out with a clear, strong voice, "I baptize you in the name of the Father and of the Son and of the Holy Spirit."

Cries of joy erupted behind Simon and echoed off the stone walls. Ella's tears trailed in shining lines down her smiling cheeks.

Simon looked around with relief to see that everyone seemed to be enjoying the moment, even Spence and Jack. He didn't know what was wrong between his two friends, but he hoped it wouldn't last long.

"Welcome to the family, Ella!" Charity said with a quick hug. It was an hour later, and everyone was gathered around Ella. Simon marveled at the changes in Charity since he had met her a year ago. Nothing too dramatic—just little surprises in ways she would reach out to others. Simon didn't know the reason behind it (or if he was just noticing it more), but he was glad to see Charity embrace Ella. After all, there had been plenty of reasons for Charity to doubt Ella's motives for wanting to be a part of the City. Simon himself had wondered about her at first.

"Hey, Simon. Have you seen Malachi lately? I wish he could have been here." Ella's question had no hint of accusation, but Simon felt guilty anyway.

"No. I haven't seen him for months," Simon replied. *When I told him I hated him. When I told him I didn't want to see him anymore.* Simon avoided eye contact with the friends who surrounded him. He remembered the deep, calm voice of Malachi—a voice he heard in some of his darkest hours. Then he remembered another voice, the dying voice of his father, struggling through pain and shallow breaths. Simon's heart turned to lead, and he pushed any thought of Malachi from his mind.

Chapter Three

The skies were dark, the air thick. Up the street, the flashlight of a Security guard whipped menacingly over walls, windows, sidewalks. A trained ear could hear the subtle thud of a Bot on patrol a few blocks away. None of this concerned him; he had nothing to fear. Walking straight down Merchant Street, he turned to his left and looked at building 2350. A long, thin smile stretched across his face as he reached into his pocket and pulled out a key.

Closing the front door behind him, he waited for his eyes to adjust to the deeper darkness. *This must be the workshop*, he thought as he walked toward the door on the left. The door groaned open, and a silent bell waved slowly in the air. The room was empty. He had no doubt that residents of the street and former customers had taken the earliest opportunity to rid the space of its worktables, chairs, and tools.

His leather boots padded softly across the room. According to what he had been told, the secret exit was along the east wall. A door that led to what appeared to be a storage room jutting from the main wall gaped ajar. *Here we are*, he smiled.

The storage room was bare except for a few cans of varnish past their prime. There was nothing—and no sign of another door. He looked around for clues to a secret panel of some sort, but the shadows concealed the corners and edges of the space. He needed illumination.

With the flip of a switch, he brought his small battery-powered lantern to life. His pale green eyes searched the room up and down. *Aha!* Metal runners on the back wall revealed the secret of one of the shelves. He slowly pushed it to the side, uncovering a small metal portal, similar to others in so many in the old buildings of this corner of the city. Instead of its original purpose of allowing for coal deliveries, it had accommodated no telling how many illegal transactions. Indignation welled up inside him as he considered the outright defiance Jonathan Clay committed against New Morgan. Against his family. Somewhere overhead, scurrying feet interrupted his thoughts. Upstairs. Yes. It was time to pay a visit to apartment 2A.

"Do you ever miss it?"

"What's that?"

"Do you ever miss your home?" Simon heaved a cardboard tray full of canned food onto a stack of others. It was Monday morning, and there was much work to do. The neediest of the Messengers had received a week's worth of food over the weekend, and other Messengers had brought in items from the meager surplus they had. It was time to reorganize the food pantry for the week. Some goods would be distributed to Messengers next weekend. Some would be used to feed the residents of the City, most of whom had nowhere else to go and no way of purchasing food from the shops aboveground.

Charity went through a crate of jars, eyeing the dates on each one. Not that it mattered. Food was rarely wasted unless undeniably spoiled.

"It was so long ago, I don't remember much. Just images here and there, and sometimes I wonder if I even remember it right," she said in a matter-of-fact tone.

Simon didn't say anything. After a moment, she continued.

"Many of the memories were hard anyway. I don't think I remember a time when my father was well. There are a few good memories, though. And it was home, you know?"

"Tell me the good memories," Simon pressed. He wanted to hear some of Charity's happiness, but he wasn't sure if it was more for her sake or his own.

As Charity tossed her head back in concentration, her long bangs fell away from her face. "My mom sang. She had a lovely voice. I don't remember what she sang exactly. But sometimes, when we all sing together on Saturday nights, some of the songs feel so familiar that I'm sure I must have heard her sing them."

Simon nodded. He remembered the first time he heard the Messengers sing and pray together. The familiar words had roused him from a very deep darkness.

"She liked to draw. We would sit together at the kitchen table, drawing. We would draw on the backs of receipts, envelopes, anything. I think we even drew on the table itself from time to time." Charity smiled at this, and Simon understood now more than ever Charity's need for creativity, her passion for art.

"I'm not sure if my mom had hobbies," Simon admitted. "Dad told me lots of things, but he didn't talk about Mom very often."

"You know," Charity said, wiping dust from a jar, "I bet some people around here remember her. Maybe you could ask them."

Simon hadn't thought about that before. The idea sent a thrill of excitement through him, and a sense of fear. Talking to others about his mom could lead to pain and anger just as much as it would lead to discovery.

"Yeah, maybe." He grabbed another cardboard tray of cans from the floor and set it on top of the stack.

"You could ask Zeke, Mrs. Meyer, even Malachi—"

A crash to the floor interrupted her, and Simon stared at a heap of dented cans where his tower had once been. Cans of green beans rolled lazily in various directions. He groaned loudly and kicked a can of fish away as it rolled toward his foot.

More startling was the noise behind him. It started low and rippled through the air with an unexpected warmth. Simon pivoted toward Charity, whose laughter shook her shoulders and broke her porcelain-doll face into a radiant smile. Simon's rising indignation foundered when he felt his own laughter build up in waves until it surfaced to his own wide grin. He realized in an instant how much he needed this moment and allowed deep laughter to shake him free.

"I'm bored."

Jack lay sprawled on the counter of the cellar, facing the ceiling. Ella sat inside the Bot, fastening a panel into place, concealing the machinery under it.

"We haven't had a mission in weeks!" he protested again.

Simon busied himself sorting metal parts in a new box of discarded pieces. He, too, ached for an excuse to feel the exhilaration of a midnight adventure—to feel the breeze, to see the stars, to share the Word. But it seemed as if the dry spell that kept the first half of August in an uncomfortable haze was holding steady. No new instances of the Message had been found.

"We haven't found it all, have we?" Simon already knew the answer, but he couldn't help but ask to fill the void. The Elders had been careful to teach all Messengers the books of the Bible. More than just an exercise, it was an imperative: a constant checklist of the Message still absent from their grasp.

"Maybe we've found all that Westbend has to offer," Ella suggested quietly.

"Wait. Wait a second!" Jack's volume started to grow. "That's it!" He sat up excitedly, and Simon couldn't understand why this news was so invigorating. "Maybe you're right, Ella. Maybe Westbend is done, at least for now. . . . But there are other cities of New Morgan, you know."

Realization dawned on Simon as he recalled the map of New Morgan in his room. Surrounded by mountains and water, New Morgan had three main cities. Port Lest was on the eastern coast and would be difficult to reach easily. But Centra wasn't too far away, was it? Were there Messengers in Centra too? *Why haven't we thought of this before?*

"So, what do we do?" Simon asked, ready to go immediately.

"Well, you can't just go by yourselves," Ella protested. "You'll need help. And probably permission, right?"

"We need to talk to the Elders." Simon sighed right after he said it. This wasn't going to be easy, and they hadn't even left yet.

Simon knew the Elders, and he had no reason to fear meeting with them, but the thought of speaking in front of their council spread an uneasiness throughout his body. The first time he'd met with them had been a dismal failure. Besides, what would he and Jack say? *What if the Elders said no? What if they said yes?*

"We can't wait any longer," Jack had decided. Simon and Jack told Zeke they had a question for the Elders, and a meeting was set for Thursday night. The two walked slowly through the mosaic hall and knocked on the door.

"Come in!" The sound was muffled, and Jack hesitated to turn the knob.

"Come, I say!" Zeke's voice was louder this time, and maybe just a bit annoyed.

Jack and Simon hurried through the doorway. Ten chairs were filled, leaving two for them to have a seat.

Johann had his back to the far wall, where the entrance to the chapel hid. Simon remembered how patient he had been during Simon's first night in the City. Cyril, sitting a few chairs to Johann's left, gave them an encouraging smile as they approached the table. Simon looked around at these leaders, these servants, these shepherds—their ages and faces varying widely from one another.

Johann cleared his throat as the two sat down. "Zeke tells us that you have a question of us," he prompted.

Jack straightened up, assuming an air of confidence, but Simon could see his right knee bouncing in nervousness.

"Simon and I, we're Carriers. We carry the Message around Westbend, to the City, to the Archives . . . but you know all that." Jack let out an awkward chuckle before continuing. "Except not anymore. I mean, we're still Carriers, of course, Mi—I mean, Simon and I are."

Simon swallowed hard. The mistake was innocent enough, but Jack turned bright red. Any mention of Micah could ruin everything.

"What Jack means is, we haven't had any missions lately. And we're assuming other Carriers haven't either. Except I guess we don't know that for sure."

Simon's pulse suddenly quickened. What if other Carriers had missions? Were he and Jack being ignored?

Jack must have had the same realization because he cast a nervous glance at Simon for a second.

"Quite right," Zeke confirmed, offering some relief.

"So, we're wondering," Jack chimed in, "what if we've found everything? I mean, I know we haven't found all the Scriptures yet, but what if we've found everything that's in Westbend? Could we find more somewhere else? Like maybe Centra?"

"What is it you propose, gentlemen?" Johann asked, folding his hands in front of him and leaning forward slightly.

Jack kicked Simon's foot, and Simon started in surprise. He cleared his throat as a distraction, hoping no one noticed. "Well, we thought maybe we could—I don't know. We could go to Centra. Try to find some other Messengers. Try to find the Message."

"And how do you plan to do this?" Cyril's deep voice questioned.

Simon looked at his hands in his lap. He and Jack had no clue what they were doing. The idea sounded so great a few days ago . . .

"Don't misunderstand us, young men," another Elder spoke. "We like the idea. We have discussed the idea ourselves recently." This Elder was two chairs to Simon's left. He was taller than Zeke, but not by much. His silver-black hair and steady, deep brown eyes gave him an air of wisdom.

Jack shook his head. "I guess we haven't thought this through. We'd need to take a truck or something to get there, right?"

Johann nodded. "Vehicles travel the single road to Centra. During the day, trucks are likely to be searched at various checkpoints. During the night, any travel is highly restricted, and every vehicle is, therefore, suspicious. Elder Chin has traveled there recently for business and made contact with others he'd known years ago. We'd like to explore this option, but we need help."

Chin, the Elder who had spoken up a moment before, turned to them, his dark eyes studying them. "This is extremely dangerous, of course, and we hesitate to ask anyone to join me."

"We'll do it!" Jack nearly shouted. "We don't have anything to lose."

The truth of this statement kicked Simon's gut, especially as he recalled his dad's old question: *What is there to lose?* He'd already lost everything.

"He's right." Simon nodded. "We'll go."

"There's just . . . one more thing," Johann inserted. "Simon, after what happened to you a few months ago, are you in the condition to face another challenge such as this? And Jack—"

All eyes turned to the recent Preparatory School graduate, his eager smile fading slightly in anticipation of what questions might come.

"We understand what Simon told us about Micah. Not everyone in the City knows the details, but I imagine plenty are wondering. You . . . you were very close to Micah, were you not?"

Jack pursed his lips and closed his eyes. Simon was starting to understand how much one person's betrayal could affect others.

"I trust him."

Simon felt all eyes turn to him.

"I trust Jack. I trust Jack with my life," Simon repeated, hoping to sound confident. It was true, Simon realized. As much as Simon couldn't stand Jack when they had first met, there was no one else he'd rather go on this mission with.

"You realize," another Elder to Jack's left added, "that the community of Messengers will wonder at our decision to send Simon Clay out with the best friend of his betrayer."

"Poppycock!"

Simon smiled despite the tense moment. Zeke to the rescue.

"Who are we? Are we afraid of a few wagging tongues? I know these boys. Both of them. And I trust them too."

Chin gave a decisive clap. "That's enough for me. We'll leave Sunday night."

The next few moments went by in a blur. The Elders rose and greeted Jack and Simon. Some clapped their backs with congratulations. Others offered words of prayer and caution. Chin shook their hands but eyed them carefully.

"I'll need to speak with both of you first thing tomorrow morning. There is much to do."

The two nodded in response and walked out together, bewildered.

"Jack?" Simon asked as he stared at the mosaic face of a stoic, green-eyed angel. "What did we just do?"

Chapter Four

"Ummm, Simon? I need a place to crash tonight."

This was the second night in a row Jack had made this request. Thursday night, it made sense. The Elders' decision and Elder Chin's insistence to meet the next morning meant that Jack had little time to leave and then return to the City. After tossing Jack his quilt—the one Jack had doused a few weeks before—Simon watched his friend fall asleep remarkably fast for someone lying on a hard stone floor. Surely Jack wouldn't want the same sleeping conditions again.

"Aren't your parents going to wonder where you are?" Simon asked. It occurred to him as he asked that he knew almost nothing about Jack's life aboveground. He'd never even thought to ask before. What kind of person knew so little about a friend? Jack knew almost everything about Simon's life—not that Simon had much of a say in the matter—but he'd never even met Jack's parents.

Jack just shrugged. They were watching Mrs. Meyer's table of baked goods while she rested upstairs. Simon tried not to think about the sudden lack of energy Mrs. Meyer displayed lately. He began scooting loaves of bread forward on the table. It was Friday evening, and the south entrance would soon be busy with plenty of Messengers planning to visit. As Simon scanned the room, his eyes fell to the far corner and a familiar mural scene. He couldn't quite make out the features from this distance, but he had every detail of his mom's face memorized. Suddenly, a terrible thought occurred to him.

"Oh no. Don't tell me you're an orphan too!" Simon half regretted the words once he said them, but honestly. *Were there no teenagers with parents anymore?* He didn't think he could handle another story of death at the moment.

Jack laughed, but there was no joy in the sound. His voice fell flat and hollow. "My parents don't particularly like the fact that their son goes out into the darkness at night. Let's leave it at that."

The response left Simon with infinitely more questions, but he could tell that none would get answered at the moment. No use in pushing it.

"Fine. But we should at least look around for a cushion or something tonight."

Saturday came and went, and Jack and Simon were exhausted. They had been training the past two days with Elder Chin. In addition to studying the street map of Centra, they also stockpiled some goods from the City, ready for loading the next night. Simon wondered why they would need to donate food and clothing to the Messengers in Centra. That community was bigger than Westbend, so it must be better prepared than their own.

The part that surprised Simon the most was the exercise. Chin had led them through tunnel after tunnel Saturday afternoon until Simon thought they had to be outside Westbend's boundaries. There were no lit torches or lanterns along the way; the halls were too remote to maintain adequate light on a regular basis. The three each navigated with a flashlight, casting beams into the bleak darkness ahead. All the walking gave Simon time to think, and he reflected on just how many tunnels he'd seen in his life. The tunnel to the dungeon of Druck-Baden Manor. The tunnel to the Room of the Martyrs. The tunnel from his apartment to the storm sewer and, later, to Ella's house. The tunnel where he fell facedown in despair until Zeke found him. Each concealed different memories—both thrilling and terrifying. He even began to realize that the worst tunnels he'd gone through were the ones he'd imposed on himself. The tunnel of denial after Life Preparation Year. The tunnel of fury and pain just months ago. He wondered if he'd live his entire life underground, roaming from one dark tunnel to another.

Just when he thought they were stopping for a break, the dark passageway they were traveling opened up into a strange room. He sensed that this cavernous space was essentially a room, but there were walls that ran up and down the length, winding in and out in a mazelike pattern. *Great. More tunnels.*

"What is this place?" Jack broke the silence with a hushed voice.

Simon shined his flashlight on the walls and saw that they were unlike the stone ones they had just passed. These walls rippled with smooth, white bumps of various sizes, lined at times with long, slender . . .

"Bones!" Jack's voice was no longer hushed, and his surprise echoed off the walls. Simon stepped back, and his right hand scraped against the wall. He yelped, worried he had touched the remains of some human long gone, but he'd only felt one of the last stones in the wall behind him. In front of him, he saw the skulls of hundreds of skeletons arranged with almost artful precision. His stomach turned.

"Ummm, Chin?" Simon moaned. "Where are we?"

"These are catacombs," Chin explained. "Early in New Morgan's history, there had been incredible infighting, and countless lives were lost. Cemeteries surrounded Westbend on all sides. Eventually, there came a time of peace, but a new struggle arose several decades later. The Messengers were under attack, mainly from rogue groups, until those groups became organized. They began bullying everyone and targeting Messengers in particular. They would find anything with a cross or other religious symbol and desecrate it, one way or another. This was particularly the case in those graveyards I mentioned. Hordes of men would march over the dead. Tombstones would be broken or vandalized. Eventually, they even began digging up the shallow graves, leaving human remains scattered on the ground."

Simon looked at the skulls around him. *Was there no place to rest in New Morgan?*

"Messengers and other groups began to work at night to prevent further destruction. They moved as many bodies as they could. The Messengers chose this place as a way to protect the bodies of their fellow Messengers from being scattered and crushed."

Jack gave a slow whistle as he turned around in place. "New Morgan sure has its share of troubles, eh, Chin?"

Chin shrugged. "New Morgan is no different from anywhere else, really. Nothing has happened here that hasn't happened elsewhere."

Simon didn't want to hear this. If he were honest with himself, he'd admit that he always held on to some hope that he could get away from New Morgan and live somewhere else, with nothing to fear ever again. He stepped closer to the wall on his right, staring into the gaping eye sockets of a skull in front of him. Out of nowhere, familiar words came to him: "the forgiveness of sins, the resurrection of the body, and the life everlasting. Amen." A wry smile pulled at Simon's cheeks. "This place is gonna be crazy on the Last Day."

"So, Chin? Why are we here?" Jack asked. His voice was uneven, and Simon knew without turning around that his friend was unnerved.

Chin responded with a question. "When was the last time you carried a Message throughout Westbend?"

Simon turned to catch Jack's grimace. "Don't remind me, man."

It had been weeks. Even before, it was a fairly slow summer, which was part of the reason they were standing in the midst of thousands of disjointed skeletons.

Chin continued. "When was the last time you ran for your life?"

That was easy: the first week of June. Charity's birthday. Just over two months ago. Simon smiled grimly—it had been the most recent time, but not the first. Probably not his last. Chin didn't wait for an audible response.

"I'm afraid to say it, boys, but you're out of practice."

A clenching in Simon's chest confirmed this statement. If they were supposed to navigate the streets of Centra, what would happen if they were caught?

Chin held up the flashlight he had been carrying. Dramatically, he turned it off. Jack and Simon didn't have to ask; they knew he expected the same from them. *Click. Click.* The pitch-black air engulfed them, and Simon felt swallowed up in death. Any movement could bring him face to bony face with a fellow saint's remains.

"What are you waiting for?" Chin's voice pierced the nothingness. "Go find the Message."

Simon took three steps and froze. The soles of his shoes squelched on the damp floor, and he could almost feel the moist grit that scraped under his feet. Even that was too loud when he was being hunted. He lifted his right foot carefully. Nothing. He set it slowly on the ground. Nothing. It would be slow going, but he knew Chin would find him in an instant if he made any noise.

Jack must have thought it through already; Simon heard nothing. His throat went dry as he realized that the only way he could prevent himself from running into a wall of bones was to hold out his hands and feel them first. *Centra isn't made of bones, is it?* Simon longed to make light of the situation with a snarky comment or joke. He longed to hear one from Jack. But the two were separated by an endless void and someone seeking to capture them.

After four steps, he was completely disoriented. Where were the bones? Two steps away? Twenty steps?

"Oooph!" Simon ran into a body, and he wasn't sure whether he was glad it was a live one.

"You're dead, Simon," Chin said quietly.

Simon let out a stream of air, and he realized he'd been holding his breath. He didn't hesitate to grab his flashlight and turn it on, figuring he could find his way to the tunnel's opening and wait.

The light, however, flashed directly into wide gray eyes.

"Aaaagh!" Jack hollered.

"And you just killed Jack," Chin added.

Simon groaned. He wanted to protest the strangeness of walking among the dead in the utter darkness to find the Word, but he had a feeling that any complaining might cost him his trip to Centra. And he still wanted to go, didn't he? Besides, he had to acknowledge that there was something fitting about this task.

"This time," Chin said, "you may use your flashlights. But remember: I can see your lights too."

Chin turned on his light and disappeared into the skeletal maze. Simon realized that he and Jack had not gotten very far at all without the light. Now, the goal would be to use it well enough while still hiding it. After a moment, Jack nodded to Simon and led the way into the heart of the room.

It felt familiar: following Jack's lead. Simon remembered how much he'd loathed Jack's cockiness in the beginning, his teasing as he led into the strange alleyways of Westbend. Jack still was annoying from time to time, but Simon meant what he had told the Elders—he trusted Jack.

Jack focused his light on the ground, and Simon's eyes could just barely make out his silhouette as he ducked, paused, and moved forward. This was better; this felt right. The two navigated the labyrinth together as a team. Like Micah and Simon. Like Micah and Jack. *Focus, Simon. Focus.*

"Found it!" Jack shouted.

A voice from a little way away called out, "Do you normally shout when you arrive at a Postmaster's home?"

Simon saw panic flash on Jack's face as he fumbled with the light and a small vial he had just pulled from underneath the gaping jaw of a skull. Jack broke into a run, failing to be as quiet as he had been before. Simon struggled to keep up, still trying to be light-footed. Jack dodged to the right around a corner.

"Oooph!"

Simon knew Jack had been caught. He darted left and sprinted away, but pain shot up his left shin. He jolted at the shock, and his right ankle twisted. He cried out as he slid on the slick floor and fell hard against a corner.

"Simon?"

Simon moaned and waved his flashlight around.

"My leg gave out on me. I dunno why." He did know. His shin had suffered several injuries, the most recent of which had been self-inflicted during a moment of rage. Malachi's face flashed in his mind as Simon remembered screaming at him and kicking a wooden crate.

Chin and Jack found Simon and started to help him up. Simon's shoe, however, hit something hard and decidedly not bonelike.

"What's this?"

Simon shined his small light around, and the beam discovered the object he'd run into—a coffin. Normally, this revelation would have earned a great deal of shock, but a coffin was comparatively less freaky than the bones that surrounded him. Still . . .

"It looks new," Simon noted. He crawled closer, his ankle and shin throbbing, and searched it for any clues as to the person inside. The coffin was secure but plain. He stood up and touched the top and felt only a thin layer of dust on it. Finally, a bright light reflected back to him as his flashlight revealed a small metal label in the center of the lid.

J. CLAY

A voice began yelling, and Simon didn't even realize it was his until he had stumbled back several steps. Between the shock, the pain, and the fact that he had bumped into a wall lined with femurs, Simon dropped to the ground and stared at the coffin. His father's coffin.

"Whoa," Jack said with awe. "Chin, did you do this?"

Simon shone the light near Chin's face and saw a look of confusion and surprise.

"I had no idea. Normally, as you know, the government takes bodies away. I hadn't heard anything about this."

"Wait a minute," Jack contested. "If the Elders didn't know about this, who did it?"

Simon knew without a doubt. His blurred memory outlined a strong silhouette carrying his father's body away.

Malachi.

Even now, after midnight worship, none of the three had breathed a word of their afternoon discovery. Simon was unnerved. If he had learned anything in the catacombs, it was that he was not ready for Centra.

Chapter Five

Unbelievable! I'm in trouble again, and it's all my brother's fault. If he had just kept his loud mouth shut, Jesus would never have known what we were talking about. Well, the other disciples wouldn't have, at least. The least. Jesus is always talking about the least. Clearly He's the greatest, and I daresay I could do some good as second in command, but Jesus won't hear of it. He doesn't seem to think I can handle it. Know this: I'll show Him. I can endure anything that comes my way for the sake of the Kingdom.

■ ■ ■

Morning came, and Simon half expected to wake to the sound of Jack's snoring, as he had the past two days. He sat up and looked over to where his friend had been sleeping: a haphazard pile of castoff cushions and a thin blanket. Jack was awake, sitting up with his back to Simon. He appeared to be reading something.

"What's that?"

Jack jumped a few inches, startled by Simon's greeting. Simon laughed heartily, enjoying his inadvertent revenge for the many times in the past when Jack had scared him. Simon stood up and crouched near his friend, who quickly composed himself.

"So when you fell and all that?" Jack started, unable to gloss over the discovery of Jonathan's coffin.

Simon nodded.

"Seconds before, we'd found the Message, remember?"

Simon had completely forgotten. After their discovery, Chin had allowed Simon to stare at the coffin for what seemed like an eternity before suggesting they head back to the heart of the City. Simon wondered now whether Chin had forgotten about the Message in the midst of the shock too, or if he simply decided to leave it alone for a while.

"So, is that it?" Simon asked, looking at the paper unrolled in Jack's hand. He noticed that Jack offered no eye roll to the obvious question. "What's it say?"

Jack cleared his throat and held up the small piece of paper.

"'For I consider that the sufferings of this present time are not worth comparing with the glory that is to be revealed to us.' Romans chapter eight, verse eighteen."

"Do we have that one in the marketplace?" Simon asked.

"I'm guessing so. I haven't heard of any new Messages lately. Plus," Jack held up the vial, "the seal was already broken."

Simon took the glass tube and examined it. It was very similar to the vials his dad had hidden in his bedroom and would take out on occasion.

"Chin must have helped translate this."

"Or carry it. Maybe he even helped find it."

Simon nodded. It was possible. Simon leaned over and read the words again. He knew that Paul had written Romans, and he knew that Paul had gone through all kinds of suffering in his lifetime.

"It kind of reminds me of Paul's Letter to the Philippians," Simon offered. Simon was well versed in the Letter to the Philippians after examining it so often a few months ago. "Especially 'to live is Christ, and to die is gain.'" Simon looked up at his door and read the words painted there.

"Sounds to me like 'What do we have to lose?'" Jack added.

Simon nodded slowly.

"We're going to Centra tonight, aren't we?"

Jack slapped Simon hard on the back. "Looks like it."

"I haven't told Charity."

"I haven't told . . . anyone either."

Simon smiled at the obvious omission of Ella's name. "Should we?"

Jack contemplated the question, and a familiar quirky smile rose to his face. "Well, no sense in worrying anyone, right? Think of the heartbreak if anything happened to us!"

Simon could see right through the bravado. Ella and Charity were two of the bravest Messengers he knew. At the same time, he knew too well the fear of losing Charity. Heartbreak didn't come close to describing it. Then, there were the other complications . . .

"And what if they told Spence?"

Jack's face turned dark. Simon waited a minute before taking a deep breath and responding to the silence.

"Look, Jack, I don't know what his problem is. I guess maybe he feels so betrayed by Micah that he doesn't want to make the same mistake again. But being suspicious of everyone isn't the answer, either."

"He isn't suspicious of everyone. He's suspicious of me. And Spence isn't the only one, you know. Aside from you, Micah was my closest friend. Everywhere I go in the City, people are staring at me, like I'm gonna just—at any minute—jump up and say, 'Surprise! I'm a mole! I'm a Judas! I've betrayed you all—ha ha ha!'"

Jack's voice rose and cracked at the end of his tirade, and he ended it by throwing his hands up in mock victory. Simon didn't miss the admission that Jack considered him a friend, but it stung a bit that they were only able to say so when things were rough. It hurt even more to know how deeply Jack had been wounded by Micah's betrayal.

"Look, Jack. I meant what I said in the Elders' room. I trust you. More than just about anyone. Do you really think I'd go to Centra on an impossible mission with someone I didn't think could handle it?"

Jack swallowed, but he said nothing. Simon took this as a win.

"Now. Get up and get outta here. This room is starting to smell like you."

"You've been quiet."

Charity placed a king on a corner and signaled a pass. The two had taken up playing cards on Sunday afternoons, and Simon appreciated the small gesture of remembering his dad.

"I'm a quiet kind of guy," Simon countered. He picked up an ace and tried not to grimace. It'd be a while before he could put that one down. He laid down a queen of hearts and jack of clubs on Charity's king of spades. His turn was over.

"Not around me, you're not!"

Simon laughed. It was true, now that he thought about it. Most of his life, he'd preferred to listen over talking, but something prompted him to act more like Jack and less like himself when it came to Charity, even from the beginning. And in recent months, the openness between them had only grown.

"What can I say? I've gotta concentrate if I'm going to win against you."

Charity set her cards down, ignoring that it was her turn.

"You know that's not what I mean," she pressed. "You weren't yourself during worship last night. I couldn't even find you Friday and Saturday. And I know you and Jack are up to something. Ella told me you were going to talk to the Elders—"

"Good ol' Ella."

"Yes! Good ol' Ella! Otherwise, I would have no idea what crazy scheme you're up to next! Even now, I don't know. Just enough to know that you're probably going to be risking your life again!"

Simon sat back. This was not the cool, calm, even aloof Charity he knew. Her green eyes flashed with anger, and her porcelain face was drawn in sharp edges.

"Charity. What can I do? I'm a Messenger—"

"So am I. So are hundreds of people here. And yet somehow, it seems like you're the only one around here who is bent on dying."

Heat rose to Simon's face, and he knew his cheeks were growing red—something new for him. Her words weren't true. He knew it, and Charity knew it. He was gearing up to list plenty of names of those who had died or were willing to die . . . but the flames in her eyes dared him to challenge her. It was no use. No logic would help at the moment. His mind raced with all kinds of arguments he could make, but nothing seemed likely to work. Thankfully, Charity must have been arguing with herself at the same time; the flames diminished to a smolder.

"Charity," Simon reasoned, trying to balance his voice between strength and empathy, "this isn't like you. I mean, you seem to take my dates with death in stride most days."

The humor worked, in a way. Charity laughed and even smiled. But the tear in her eye nearly killed him without the help of any Bots or Security or evil family members. Her words were even worse.

"It's never easy, though. And it's getting harder."

Simon's heart squeezed so hard, he knew this must be the end of him. He was hurting her. He reached over to grasp her hand, and his heart plummeted to his gut when she pulled away. But she stood. And walked toward him. Without thinking, he stood with open arms, welcoming her into an embrace. He held her tight, knowing that losing her—in addition to all he'd already lost—might almost be more than he could bear. Charity was trying to tell him that the same was true for her. He rested his chin on her head, and his eyes began to cloud with tears. Charity looked up, and Simon's world spun as she gently pulled his face down, her lips meeting his own.

Simon felt simultaneously numb and on fire. He'd been so, so careful. He knew that Charity's life before the Messengers had been a hell on earth, and he'd never wanted to do anything at all that would betray her trust in him. It had been a constant, slow asking her permission to let him into her life. Every moment was worth it, and he would never forgive himself if he ever broke her confidence in him. The kiss was just a second or two, but it was everything. It was affirmation of all they never dared to say. He looked down at her face, still taut with the stress of their conversation, but he laughed when he looked into her eyes and saw the question—the same question he was constantly asking her. *Yes. Yes, I care about you, Charity. Yes, the feeling is mutual. I thank God that the feeling is mutual.* He kissed the tear that escaped her left eye and held her close.

"Charity," Simon whispered to her, "I never want to hurt you. I don't think I could ever forgive myself if I did."

She felt so small in his arms, but he knew better than to think she was fragile or weak. Few Messengers were as strong as she was; few Messengers had endured as much as she had. Charity's shoulders relaxed with a sigh, and she pulled back to look him in the face—the challenge in her own face setting firmly back into place.

"I know you're leaving me. Just don't die."

"Charity . . ." He paused. This mission had just become infinitely more difficult. "Charity, you know I can't promise that." His will began to crumble, a mirror of the young woman who stood in front of him. He sighed and stepped back, suddenly feeling alone. He took her hand and hoped she wouldn't pull away.

"Yes, I'm leaving. God willing, I'll be back soon. And for your sake more than anything . . ." he swallowed. This new honesty between them was uncharted territory. "I'll try to come back in one piece."

Charity said nothing, but she looked down at their hands and squeezed his fiercely. He winced, but knew a cry of pain wouldn't help her confidence in his ability to face impending danger.

"Besides, who will beat you in cards?"

In a flash, Charity left him and grabbed a card. She slapped three cards on his jack, moved a seven over from a different spot, and tossed two more cards in the empty space. Charity beamed with mischief and victory.

Simon groaned. "Why do I even try?"

Chapter Six

"Ready?"

"Frankly, no."

"Ever think about how the North Gate is really more to the west?"

"Also no."

"I mean, I guess it's more north than the South Gate, but . . . it's always bothered me a little."

"Huh."

"Or maybe we can call it the Apostles Gate and then the South Gate could be the Martyrs Gate, and then—"

"Jack."

"Yeah?"

"Is it imperative that you talk right now?"

"I'd have to say . . . yes. Probably. Either that, or I'll have to start jumping up and down or something."

Simon groaned. Any minute now, Chin would meet them in the Room of the Twelve, and they would leave through the North Gate. West Gate? Whatever. It would be the point of no certain return. While Jack was flapping his jaw, Simon kept his mouth clamped shut as tightly as possible. He feared he might vomit otherwise.

"Tell me why we're doing this again," Simon allowed through clenched teeth.

"Because I was bored?"

Simon whirled at him with every intention of knocking Jack to the ground, but Jack deflected any attacks by waving his hands and talking quickly.

"No, no, just kidding. Really. Because of the Message. We seem to be out of it, and we only have . . . what? Like half of it? If this is the Message worth dying for, it's worth finding and reading and sharing too."

Simon slowly nodded, taking the response in. *Okay. This was worth it.*

Chin walked under the middle archway toward them from the marketplace. He was wearing dark clothes and a knit cap. Simon pulled the hood of his jacket over his head.

Chin gave a single nod.

"Ready?"

Michael opened the door for them, and the night flooded Simon's senses. There was a touch of coolness on the warm evening, and Simon became keenly aware of how long it had been since he breathed in fresh air. They stepped out, and Simon looked up. The sky was clear, but the moon was hidden. Stars flecked the city sky.

Wordlessly, Chin took the lead, and Jack fell behind. Simon knew that his middle position implied that he was the weakest member of the group, but he had no time for pride. He wanted to come back alive.

Despite their dismal failure in the catacombs, Simon and Jack moved in sync easily behind Chin. Simon's muscles tightened, urging him forward, eager for another adventure. Chin made his way down the short alleyway and turned south immediately. The typical zigzag pattern carried them away from the gate soon enough, but Simon imagined they were still above the City at this point. Who was just below them? Ella and Spence? Mrs. Meyer? Charity? Simon shook his head and tried to focus on Chin's silhouette ahead.

Simon began to feel a little winded and marveled at how quickly he could get out of shape. He'd have to make a habit of walking through tunnels when he got back home. *Home.* Simon's focus was blown again, and he sprinted a few steps, as if he could shake the distractions and emotions by outrunning them.

Chin began moving faster, and Simon made sure he was close behind. After two quick turns, he stopped fast when he saw Chin standing still. In front of them, a small delivery truck was parked at the end of an alley. Chin motioned them to the back of it. There was only a foot or two between the end of the truck and the brick wall at the end of the alleyway, but Chin slipped between and raised the door, which slid up with a low grumble. He motioned for Simon to get in. As Simon crawled into the back, he heard Jack's footsteps catch up. In less than a minute, all three were standing in the back of the cargo area, facing a closed door and seeing only darkness. Inches behind him, Simon could feel a wall of boxes.

"Now what?" Jack whispered.

"Now, we wait," Chin said in a low tone.

"Till when?"

"Till sunrise. Sleep tight, gentlemen."

He didn't have to open his eyes to know it was there. Roaring with mechanical fury, Maximalus was no doubt hovering over him, its metallic scorpion body threatening to crush Simon as it had ended so many inferior Bots in battle. He could even smell the fumes of spent fuel and fully expected to choke on thick, black smoke in seconds. It's a wonder he didn't scream. It's a good thing he didn't. When he finally had courage to open his eyes, he was astounded at the mundane sight around him. He was in a dark room. With boxes. But the floor underneath churned, and he realized he was moving. The truck. Yes, that's where he was. It was all coming back to him: Chin and Jack, the dark alleyways, Centra. His brief relief gave way to panic again as he knew he was not that much safer here than if he were inches away from the vicious Bot Westbend touted as its champion. He was contraband cargo on a mission to find a group of fellow outlaws in an unfamiliar city.

Without warning, Simon's muscles began to scream in pain after sleeping in such a strange position. The night before, Chin, Jack, and Simon had done their best in the dark to rearrange the trailer full of boxes so they could have enough room to sleep covertly. By restacking and moving boxes one at a time, they were able to set boxes closer to the door and make three canyons of open space, each surrounded by more boxes. The result was floor space only wide enough for each person to sit with crossed legs, separated from one another. The logic was that if one person was found, maybe the other two wouldn't be. They all knew a half-hearted search was unlikely, but it was something. Simon and Jack were concealed closer to the cab of the truck, with Simon on the driver side and Jack on the passenger side; Simon had no idea how Chin managed to finish enclosing himself within the boxes, but he had assured them he was safe.

Simon slowly moved his legs from the crouched position he had assumed all night, stretching his muscles with care. He could see the ceiling above him; his desire to stand upright instantly overcame him, and he leaned forward on his knees. He tested one foot, then the other, and he was up. Simon's hands pressed against the ceiling as he stretched every muscle from toe to fingertip. After a few minutes, the pain ebbed until he felt himself again. His left leg still throbbed a little, but he was starting to realize that the dull, nagging ache was so prevalent he rarely noticed it, unless he thought about it or the pain was more intense than usual. Simon considered that this might become a permanent reminder of the struggles he had endured at the Arena, outside City Hall, and—most of all—in the vacant building next to Ella's house.

"Simon?"

"Yeah?"

"You awake?"

Simon rolled his eyes. "Yeah."

"Next time I tell you I'm bored, smack me, all right?"

"Gladly."

"Gentlemen. I know the engine will cover our noise, but perhaps it would be best if we keep our conversation to that which is necessary."

Simon stood in the silence, staring at boxes. He wondered how close they were to Centra. How long until they could get out of the truck? He imagined security checks on the road. Alleyways and Bots. He thought of Druck. Of his grandmother.

And it had only been a matter of minutes.

"Ummm, Chin?" Jack's voice rose above the boxes. "With all due respect, I think it's necessary."

After a pause, Chin answered, "You may be right."

"Let's give it a shot. Okay, let's see. What are our chances of getting back to Westbend alive?"

Simon uttered a groan loud enough for both of them to hear.

"Not helpful? I guess not."

Simon couldn't help but chuckle a little, and he realized that Jack was acting more himself.

Chin's tone wasn't filled with the same humor. "You've all had to grow up so fast. Too fast."

"Well, Chin, I guess the bright side is that we don't know any better," Jack offered. "Until you told us. Thanks for that."

"At least you finished school, Jack," Simon confided. "I'm a nobody."

"We knew that already, Simon."

"No, really. I can't believe I'm saying this, but I wish I could go back to school this year. I want my life to be normal, like it was."

"Like when?" Jack challenged.

"What?"

"You want your life to be normal, like it was. When? When you were a criminal, sneaking out at night? When you were searching for answers to questions you didn't know to ask? When you were brainwashed and didn't even remember who the Messengers were? That was normal, all right. When you were a kid, wondering why your mom wasn't around? Let's face it, Simon. You aren't normal. You aren't supposed to be."

"All right, then," Simon countered. He didn't take time to think about what Jack said. He just wanted to have his say too. "What about you? You have parents, right? But where are they? Are they Messengers? You've finished Preparatory School, but now what? What are you going to do next? Did you pass well enough to get more training? Are you going to take on some trade? Are you going to join the military?"

"Shut up, Simon!"

Simon fell silent. Jack was mad. But was Jack ever mad, really? Maybe this talking thing was a bad idea after all. Still, silence at this point would be worse.

"So, um, Chin," Simon tried, "what about you? Where is your family?"

A brief silence dashed Simon's hope at regaining normalcy anytime soon, but Chin obliged.

"I am from a different country. You have to go to Port Lest and take a boat for three days before traveling on land again for four more days. Or at that point, you could take a plane, if you can afford it."

Simon remembered hearing about planes before, but he had never seen one.

"I was here in New Morgan—Morganland, actually—to study. I studied with your father, in fact, Simon. I had come to continue my education, and we were in the doctoral program at the seminary together. My wife, Meili, and I had three children at the time. It was difficult to be away from our home, our families, but we would soon go back. After years of hard work and making ends meet, I was finished! It was time to go home."

There was something nagging at Simon as he heard this story. It sounded too much like others he'd heard. It was a story of sacrifice and—he imagined—suffering. Chin's voice was monotone, and Simon knew it was because of Chin's effort to keep the words coming.

"We boarded the train at Westbend to go to Centra and then Port Lest. One, two, three, four. Meili and the kids went through. They stopped me at the door. This was just as New Morgan had outlawed all churches. Your father may have told you, Simon."

He had. Simon remembered his dad telling him about all the changes his parents had witnessed in their early years—their only years. He knew the seminary was nothing but rubble now.

"They detained me. Meili screamed for me, but I warned her with a look that I hoped would keep her silent, and safe. I told myself they'd only keep me a few days and I could catch up with my family, but after four days of questioning, they decided I was a spy. The only way they would let me remain alive was if I stayed here, within their boundaries and under their watch."

Chin's voice had retained control most of the story, but it was breaking now. Simon tried to picture Chin's wife and kids back home, but without Chin. How old would they be? Older than Simon was now.

"Chin, you're a warrior, man." Jack's voice was strained as well. Simon was somewhat grateful for the boxes that kept them separate. Simon's own eyes were blurring at the countless lives changed forever because of New Morgan.

"Have . . . have you heard from them?" Simon dared to ask, regretting it almost instantly.

The truck engine rumbled underneath the deafening silence.

Chapter Seven

The truck drove on, and Simon eventually sat again. The quiet monotony began lulling him back to sleep until the tenor of the motor deepened, slowed, and stopped.

What happened? Are we there? Is it safe? Are we stopped? Are we caught? Simon wanted to ask all these questions out loud, but he knew that it could mean the difference between freedom and capture, between life and death.

Simon strained his ears to hear, but the sounds of traffic passing by drowned out anything discernable. He heard muffled voices. One stern and abrupt, the other low and calm, almost familiar. A sharp rapping on the trailer wall would have caused Simon to jump up had he not been frozen in place. He imagined Jack and Chin in their own isolated spaces, waiting for what was to come.

The rapping continued down the length of the truck. The pounding in Simon's ears matched the pulse of whoever was coming to find them, banging on the metal toward the back. The door screamed as it pulled open on rusty wheels. Simon detected a change in light on the roof and held his breath. The screeching stopped. Simon didn't think the door could have been completely open yet, but what was wrong? Why did they stop? One voice demanded as much, from what Simon could tell over another vehicle roaring past. The door wrenched twice, shuddering under emphatic tugs, but nothing happened. A shout of frustration came from the impatient voice. Simon heard it coming for a few moments: a truck maybe twice the size of the one they were stowed inside barreled past, shaking the vehicle around them. In what sounded like a string of curses, the angry voice joined the sounds of the door as it shrieked back in place. Eerie stillness laid heavy on Simon until the familiar motor revved and began moving them forward again.

After a few moments, Chin began humming a tune. Simon didn't recognize it, but it sounded calm and reverent; Simon knew without asking that he was listening to a doxology.

Simon didn't dare fall asleep anymore, and the monotony that once lulled him now grated on his nerves. Could they be sure they were going to Centra? Who was driving, anyway? Could they trust him? Could they trust anyone? The fact that they were still alive had to be something, right? Simon pictured the truck pulling over again, but this time, the door would open. A line of guards would be waiting, guns in hand. Chin, Jack, and he would walk toward the ditch on the side of the road, just like . . . just like . . . Simon suddenly broke into a sweat, and nausea swept over him. He bent over and breathed slowly, willing himself to calm down. The deep brown eyes of his mother's likeness stared at him, and he moaned with the effort to keep it together.

"Simon? Hey, man, you okay?"

Simon could only groan in reply. The boxes that surrounded him appeared to be closing in on him, and he was sure he'd be swallowed up any minute, breathless and alone.

"'For I consider,'" Jack spoke up to the ceiling, his voice reflecting down to Simon, "'that the sufferings of this present time are not worth comparing with the glory that is to be revealed to us.' Romans chapter eight, verse eighteen."

Simon smiled. He took a long, slow breath.

"'The LORD is on my side,'" Chin added. "'I will not fear. What can man do to me?' Psalm one eighteen, verse six."

Jack took another turn. "'The LORD is my light and my salvation; whom shall I fear? The LORD is the stronghold of my life; of whom shall I be afraid?' Psalm . . . Psalm . . .'"

"Twenty-seven," Chin helped.

"Right. Thanks."

Simon looked up to the ceiling and pulled words of comfort from his own memory.

"'Though I walk through the valley of the shadow of death, I will fear no evil, for You are with me.' Psalm twenty-three. I used that one in the dungeon of Druck-Baden Manor." He let the silence fall as he pictured the dark hallway, the cold, stone room. The piercing eyes of Mr. Druck, his mother's own brother.

"We've seen a lot of evil, haven't we?" he asked the others. He knew their silence was affirmation as they relived whatever horrors they had endured.

"Sometimes I think about what I was like just a year ago. Everything was normal, plain, boring. I wanted so badly to uncover all the mysteries of New Morgan. I knew there had to be something more real underneath all the gray plaster. I didn't realize there was more underneath my own memories too. I've learned the truth, for sure, both good and evil."

"Do you regret it?"

"What do you mean?" Simon asked.

Jack repeated himself slowly. "Do you regret it? Do you wish you still knew nothing?"

Simon paused. He'd seen so much in his life. And yet, he knew his life had been empty, hollow, when the Message was buried deep inside him, covered over with pain and walls and fog. He knew that the only thing that gave him purpose lately was the Word, the λόγος. New Morgan had done everything in its power to conceal it forever, but that still was not enough. The Messengers would find the truth, and they would reveal it no matter the cost.

He smiled as he repeated the words they discovered not far from his father's body.

"'For I consider that the sufferings of this present time are not worth comparing with the glory that is to be revealed to us.'"

The truck began making stops and turns, so Simon figured they had made it to Centra. Relief washed over him: they were here. But Simon had no idea how much longer it would take to get to their destination. He stood and stretched, facing the inside of the cargo area, but a sudden turn caused him to lose his bearings. He fell forward, knocking the box on the top toward the center of the truck. The box hit the one next to it, which produced a noisy clank on its way down.

"Owwwwww!" The half yelp, half whisper from Jack emanated pain and frustration.

"Sorry," Simon whispered.

Jack groaned. "You'd better be thankful that wasn't full of cans or something."

Chin shushed them both. The box close to Simon began shifting back in place as Jack pushed his own box where it belonged. Simon kept a hand out to keep it from falling his way, just in case Jack was in the mood for retribution.

With little warning, the truck slowed to a stop and the engine died. Silence. After a few minutes, Simon dared to whisper.

"Chin? Are we here?"

"I suspect so."

"So, umm, what do we do now?"

"Well, it's still daylight. For now, we wait."

Silence again.

Jack took his turn to speak, "So, is there anything to eat?"

"I suggest you carefully look through the boxes near you, but keep it to a minimum; we don't have much in the way of amenities here."

"Oh man," Jack groaned. "You mean we gotta hold it till sundown?"

Simon closed his eyes. "Just try not to think about it."

"But I am thinking about it."

"Jack? Remind me never to go on a trip with you again."

"Gentlemen, may I remind you that there is no motor to cover up our voices?"

Simon sat back down and attempted the best thing he could think of to pass the time: sleep. Before closing his eyes, he looked up to the ceiling and offered a prayer for them, for Centra, and for loved ones far away.

When Simon woke, his muscles throbbed, his tongue was swollen, and his stomach growled. He smelled of sweat, and he had to go to the bathroom. To make matters worse, he realized within moments why he woke up. The door had opened, and he had no idea who had jumped into the truck, causing the floor to dip momentarily with the added weight. His heart raced, wondering if he would have the strength to fight against any intruders. It sounded like there were at least two men, talking quietly and unloading the boxes one by one.

"Chin? Is that you?"

Simon heard Chin's fatigued voice reply, "It is. Good to see you, Zane."

"Chin, you look terrible. Let's get you off of this truck."

"There are others. We need to get them out."

Simon didn't even bother getting up at first. He was concerned that if he stood too quickly, he would lose control of his balance. Or worse. Once the top box to his right was pulled away, he slowly began to get up.

"Easy there, buddy. Hey, how long were you all in here?!"

The man who spoke was large; the short sleeves of his black shirt stretched against his arms. His brown eyes matched his hair, which seemed to be everywhere. Thick, messy curls sat on top of his head, and his beard was long and full.

"Whoa, Zane, you've gotta come over here."

The bearded man turned his head to Jack's side of the truck and walked toward his partner, whom Simon could not see.

"Oh boy. This isn't good."

Simon leaned out into the open area and saw two men—one of them Zane—lift Jack up. As the two led him on either side, Jack stared blankly in Simon's direction. Large, dark circles surrounded his eyes, and he stumbled even with the support of Zane and his friend.

"No, you can't take me to the military. Simon. Simon won't make me go, right, Si? Clay? No. He won't make me. Can't go."

"Easy now. Down we go."

Simon had no idea who these people were, but they knew Chin. And they had Jack—who clearly was in worse shape than he was. Slowly, he crawled out of the back of the truck and let himself down onto the pavement below. The sky was dark, and the air was cool and damp. He looked up and saw the stars blinking down on him—the same stars that were over Westbend. *Look at the stars.* Malachi's voice drifted through Simon's mind. They could probably use Malachi's help right now, but he was nowhere to be seen. *It's my fault.* Simon tried to swallow, but a hard lump nearly choked him. With relief, he noticed that the four others were ducking into a door just ten feet away. When he entered, he found a beautiful sight: a bare room with a few pillows, a jug of water, and an open door that revealed a toilet.

"You all stay here," Zane told them. "Garrett and I will take care of the truck. We'll come back before dawn."

It didn't matter that Simon had just passed most of the day asleep; he felt exhausted, and he was more than happy to wait out his next hours in Centra with more than a box-width of living space. But first things first.

"Jack? You okay?"

Simon was up and feeling relatively refreshed. Jack was still asleep, but he was looking better after Chin and Simon insisted he drink plenty of water for the first few hours. Chin lay flat on the floor, facedown, and Simon waited as he prayed. Simon sat against the wall, arms around his knees, and he lifted his eyes to the ceiling.

"I lift up my eyes to the hills." Simon silently meditated on the familiar words, words that had brought him peace long ago. "From where does my help come? My help comes from the LORD, who made heaven and earth."

Simon closed his eyes. He didn't know what words could possibly do justice to all his thoughts and concerns, but he also knew that didn't matter. Thoughts and words tumbled in his mind as he prayed. He prayed for Charity. For Ella. For Mrs. Meyer. For Spence. For all the Elders. For Chin. For Jack. He paused and thought about Malachi. Where was he? Did he need help? *And Lord*, Simon prayed, *forgive me for what I said to Malachi. I'm still hurt. I'm still angry. But* . . . Simon sighed, feeling the truth lift another weight from his shoulders. *But I'm not angry with Malachi. He should be angry with me. If I get the chance, help me apologize to him.* Simon felt the sting of old wounds reopening, and he was tempted, so tempted, to cover them back up, to retreat into the old fog that numbed his pain. But, as Simon knew, the cloudy haze also concealed truth. He continued to pray, and he felt tears roll down his face. Slowly, a balm worked into the cracked crevices of his heart and gave bittersweet relief.

When Simon opened his eyes, Chin was up and silently moving around the room, stretching his body in an orchestrated routine.

"We should exercise," Chin said when Simon stood up. "But we must be careful. Before we do much, we will need food."

"Chin? Those boxes in the truck. What were they for?"

"Many of them were filled with the food we brought for Centra. Others deep in the trailer were empty."

"Those would have been nice in the front, where we had to move them all around."

"Empty boxes during a security raid would have been a red flag, to be sure."

Simon nodded. "Who loaded the food boxes?" While he'd helped with them in the City, they were already in the trailer during their midnight escape.

Chin continued to stretch. "I had help Saturday night. Come, move your muscles."

Simon slowly stretched, trying to mimic half of Chin's movements. Every muscle in his body protested with even the smallest effort, but the work felt like progress. With confidence, Simon reached behind his back and clasped his hands, bending forward with his arms straight behind him. His vision blurred, and he saw blue stars.

"Watch me," Chin said sternly. Simon sheepishly complied.

A groan from the floor stopped both Chin and Simon as they watched Jack rub his eyes with his fists.

"Did that truck hit me or something?"

Before Simon could respond, a click behind him drew their attention to the opening door. Garrett walked in, holding a tray of food. Zane followed behind with a new jug of water.

"Sorry we took so long," Garrett said, placing the tray on the floor near Jack. "Thought you'd be ready to eat."

Simon looked at the assortment of dried fruit, crackers, and a few small pieces of cured meat. Simon thought this might be his favorite meal ever.

"Dig in, guys," Zane encouraged, sitting cross-legged on the floor. "We have some questions for you."

Chapter Eight

The apartment lay ridiculously bare. Any idiot could see that the Darkness had swept through immediately to rid the place of any evidence. *The boy's father was likely still cooling with death when those pests invaded the place,* he thought grimly. *And they think they're so much smarter than the rest of us.*

He paced the kitchen, his hands examining the counter, certain he would find some sort of lever or latch that would expose the secrets he sought to find. Nothing. Just a photo on the side of the refrigerator he dared not look at.

On the east side of the spacious room, shapes on the floor indicated where rugs and furniture had once sat, protecting the floorboards from the sun. He flashed his light over the boards, stamped on the floor, and even lowered himself to his knees to inspect the area.

Nothing.

The boy's bedroom was obviously the one with the east window. He peered out, eyeing the alley below. He could see the place where his mother had evidently waited those first nights after the Arena, certain she could catch them leaving their portal and leading her straight to their headquarters. She didn't admit it, but they both knew she had failed. He would not. This would be his opportunity to show her the son he was. He drew near to the mirror on the north wall and smiled. His straight white teeth and carefully groomed dark hair suited him well. Even if he looked Revemondian. Well, what of it? His name told everyone who he was, and he was well suited for it. Roderick Druck Jr. If his father could see him now, he would be proud. He was sure of it. Once he found their lair . . .

He walked into the traitor's bedroom, and his patience began to wane. Pictures of her were everywhere, taunting him. This was the fourth time in as many weeks that he had searched this apartment, and he wasn't going to come out empty-handed. Not. This. Time.

The furniture in this room was largely untouched, which baffled him. The bed took up much of the room, which only meant a search was more difficult. With mounting frustration, he heaved at the mattress, shoving it off the other side of the bedframe. Nothing. Angry now, he began stamping on the floorboards. With a particularly flippant kick near the dresser, his foot slid and caused him to be completely unbalanced, landing hard on his posterior. He nearly hollered out in rage, but something caught his eye: the floorboard. The reason his foot gave way was because the board had moved, sliding right up and out of its place.

"Aha!" he cried out to no one. He scrambled to the rectangular hole in the ground and peered in. Into darkness. Into nothingness. In desperation, he shoved his hand into the space, but was rewarded only with a small, sharp pain. He'd been bitten by something lurking in the shadows. Spewing a stream of curses, he leaped back up, shaking his hand. Her portrait sat on top of the dresser, laughing at him, mocking him. He snatched the frame and smashed it against the wall.

"Take that, Abigail! You can't stop me now!" Druck sneered.

Her face stared back at him, and he grabbed at the loose photograph, intent to finish the job of destroying her smug smile. The photo had been taken outside, in a courtyard of some kind. But where was she? He turned the picture over and smiled. "Abigail, age 24" was written in faded cursive handwriting. Under it were two more words, but the pencil lead was so aged, it was nearly impossible to see. He shone his flashlight onto it and squinted. Slowly, he recognized the letters. *That's it!* A long, hearty laugh escaped from his lips, and he didn't care who could hear him.

"So, Chin," Zane said as he scratched at his beard, "why did you all come to visit? The food is certainly appreciated, but this can't be just a charity run."

Simon's heart thudded rapidly at the accidental mention of her name. Where was Charity? Was she safe? Was
she worried? Was she angry?

Chin finished chewing his bite of fruit and placed his
hands on his knees. He had adopted Zane's cross-legged
posture, but Simon was adamant to keep his legs as
stretched out as possible.

"It did seem as though you could use supplies. I had
spoken with Glen when I visited recently, and he told
me of your struggles here."

"I don't get it," Simon interrupted. "Centra is way bigger
than Westbend, right? So your Messengers headquarters
have to be way bigger! I mean, you're all more organized
and everything, right? Why wouldn't you be?"

Chin looked at Simon without expression, and Simon
just realized he'd made a fatal mistake. Ever since they
escaped the truck, Simon had assumed that these two
were fellow Messengers, but what if they weren't? What
if they were just nice for some other unknown reason,
and now they were going to take them to the authorities?
What if—

"You'd think so," Zane conceded, running a hand
through his messy curls. "But a bigger city means a bigger
government. And Centra is the capital, so Security is more
keen than ever to show that all-powerful New Morgan is
unchallenged. Boy, we heard that Westbend had a bit of
an uprising not too long ago. That one lady . . . Durke?
Drake? Druck. Yeah, Bander-Druck or something. She's
in charge of suppressing the Darkness in Westbend. She
was all over our papers, saying how everything's just

fine. That must've been something, eh? Bet she got into some trouble!"

Simon didn't feel as talkative anymore.

"That's not the only thing," Garrett added from across the room. He was standing, leaning half of his body against the wall. "Westbend is an older city. Sounds like you have old tunnels and things, right? Well, Centra is not as old. The architecture is not nearly as exciting. Or easy to navigate from a covert perspective."

Simon's disappointment in Centra must have been evident. Zane actually came over and patted Simon's head before sitting down again near Jack, who was listening quietly. Simon tried not to take the gesture as patronizing, but he couldn't help feel a little annoyed with the first resident of Centra he'd met. On the other hand, he was glad Zane thought to check on Jack.

"And the worst part, really," Garrett continued, "is that we don't even know how many of us are out there. You know. Messengers. That's what you call yourselves, right? Believers?"

Simon nodded, his heart sinking. Why did they come here at all? *What was the point?*

"When it comes to apathy, Centra was riddled with it. People barely noticed when the Word became illegal. Half of them were glad, convinced it was some sort of old-fashioned, backward document of hate or something. At least that's what they were told."

"By the government?" Simon asked.

"Nah. By each other."

"Did they even try to read it?"

"They didn't even bother," Garrett answered.

Simon was about to get indignant when Jack cut in, surprising them all.

"Just like the Maxons, Simon. At least in part. All sorts of people just stopped caring."

It was hard to be angry when he could put faces to those who had ignored God's Word. If he was honest, he knew his own face belonged in that group as well.

"We're glad the food can help," Chin inserted.

"Oh yes. There are plenty in need," Zane replied. "We make runs at night to deliver rations to Messengers who need extra food—but to anyone, really. It's not pretty around here. I'm sure you have the same in Westbend, but maybe it's worse in a place with more people and more restrictions. People are starving."

Simon considered this. Westbend Messengers carried the Word. Centra Messengers carried food. Westbend Messengers showed mercy by using Grand Station as a hub for distributing goods. Centra Messengers . . . didn't even know how big their community was. He had been hoping they would receive help from Centra, not the other way around.

"We were hoping you might be able to help us as well," Chin continued his train of thought, matching with Simon's.

Garrett nodded.

"Sure. We don't have much food, but we have stockpiles of all kinds of other things. Warehouses and factories just sit there, with all kinds of things rusting and rotting in place. There's a huge industrial area that is nothing but shells of buildings now. We keep what we can, but people need only so much paint and metal."

"Thank you," Chin responded. "That would help, no doubt. And the boxes would do a fine job concealing us when we return to Westbend. But that is not why we came. We are seeking the most precious resource." After a pause, he clarified, "We are seeking the Word. The λόγος."

There was an awkward pause. "I thought you had it," Zane answered, confusion written on his face. "That's the rumor, anyway. Westbend Messengers have the Word and are sharing it. Isn't that why there was an uprising in the first place?"

Simon couldn't believe how much news of his actions had spread. He hadn't any idea that Centra knew what was happening in his corner of the world.

"You could say that," Jack answered. "Simon was behind most of the sharing part of it. That's why we took him on this mission. He's crazy."

Danger brought out the best in Jack, and Simon welcomed it.

"The truth is," Chin answered Zane, "we have some of it. We've been desperately trying to find everything we can, and when we do, it's usually in the original languages, which is why those documents survived. But we don't have everything, and passages are getting increasingly difficult to find. We were hoping you might have some portions of the Word as well."

"Glen has some, but we don't have near the operation you all have," Garrett answered. "He's our only pastor right now. There might be others somewhere, but we don't know who they are."

"I don't get it," Simon protested. He was starting to learn he couldn't make assumptions about Centra, but this seemed ridiculous. "We have a lot of pastors, and some of them form a group to help lead us in the mission to find the Word. They're called Elders. Can't this Glen, like, remember other pastors who were pastors before New Morgan came about? Ask them to join up?"

"You don't know much about Centra's history, do you?" Garrett countered with a bit of an accusation. "And clearly, you don't know how dangerous it can be to be a pastor."

Simon clouded over, and it took all the willpower he had to keep from charging Garrett and bolting out of this room. This whole mission was a waste of time, and they were trapped in a room with people who didn't know much of anything—least of all what Simon did or didn't know.

"Maybe your pastors are just cowards," Simon spat. He knew it was heartless as soon as he said it, but he felt a bit of righteous indignation at anyone who would imply that Westbend's pastors didn't know sacrifice.

"Whoa, Clay, easy," Jack cut in. "Uh, Garrett? I'm sure you're right that we have a lot to learn about your pastors. And—dare I say it—vice versa. It'd be helpful for you to know, for example, that Simon's dad, a pastor, was killed about four months ago. And as far as New Morgan is concerned, Simon doesn't exist anymore. So let's all just take a moment and acknowledge how much this whole place stinks, eh?"

Simon almost laughed. Jack's easygoing tone sounded ludicrous in the situation, but in a way, that was perfect. This whole situation, this whole country was ludicrous.

"Sorry, man," Garrett said after a moment. "I lost my head."

"Yeah, I tend to do that a lot lately," Simon confessed. His realized that he had been clenching his jaw. And he knew in that moment that if he had been looking in the mirror as he attacked Garrett, he would have seen a face like Ben's. Like Micah's.

"Gentlemen, I'm afraid we're running out of time," Chin said. "Is Glen anywhere nearby?"

"Not exactly," Zane replied. "But we can take you to him, as long as you all feel strong enough." He looked pointedly at Jack.

Jack clapped his hands and rubbed them together. "Well, what are we waiting for?"

Chapter Nine

Simon was out of shape, no doubt about it. Granted, he had been trapped inside of a truck for a day, and the group of five had been weaving in and out of buildings for much longer than a typical Carrier run. Still. Chin was darting, jogging, and ducking right along with Garrett and Zane. Simon and Jack were wheezing and stumbling. Simon half expected Chin to tell them to wait in some alleyway cranny until they came back. Or until they were caught. But at the rate they were going, getting caught was likely either way. Simon did notice with gratitude that there weren't many flashlights or footsteps from Security to dodge. And as for Bots . . .

Thud, thud, thud.

Simon would have groaned if his life didn't depend on it.

Garrett darted to the opposite side of the alley, motioning to Jack to follow suit. Zane nodded to Chin and Simon to stay with him. Everyone cowered behind crates and refuse bins. One thing Simon definitely noticed: Centra was filthy, much worse than Westbend. Maybe this lack of attention would mean people could get away with more, but that didn't seem to be the case if the underground church was any indication.

Thud, thud, thud.

It was strange, but he no longer felt the panic he had known so well when he traveled the streets with Micah and Jack. Fear was still there, and in many ways, there was more at stake than before. But danger had become as familiar to him as calm. Really, it was more familiar. Like a seasoned warrior, he embraced the adrenaline of battle, knowing what they were fighting for.

Thud, thud, thud.

Simon snapped out of his musings and pressed himself against the brick wall to his left. He peered at the street at the end of the alley and took in the features of a new Bot. Four powerful legs held up a massive body. The creature looked almost like an elephant, but without the ears. In place of a trunk, a long, narrow cannon protruded from a swiveling head. Simon held his breath. As dangerous as each Bot was, this was the first he had seen with a long-range weapon.

The metallic beast paused at the alley, and its head slowly scanned back and forth across the intersection. Zane held his arm out against Simon, pushing him even closer against the wall. He bent his head down without moving forward and looked at the ground. Simon assumed the same position, keeping his eyes away from the machine. Suddenly, blinding light flooded the alley.

Simon could only guess that the source of the beam was the Bot's head. Simon knew they would be discovered; there was no way they could be overlooked. Slowly, the light retreated and moved toward the alley on the other side. Simon dared to turn his face in the Bot's direction and—could it be? His eyes must still be adjusting, but there, in the center of the alley, appeared a lone silhouette, the size of a large man. The Bot must have detected something too; it maneuvered toward the shadow, but the figure was moving quickly, silently. The cannon raised, aimed, and fired. The sound was deafening, no doubt waking any resident in a two-block radius. The distinct smell of propellant, along with dust and debris, billowed along the length of the alley. Simon suppressed a cough and risked a look in the direction of the Bot's target. Through the dust, he could see the light searching down the alley, but nothing was there. Though his ears were still ringing, Simon could hear the metallic groan of the machine as it resituated and began thudding its way down the street.

After the sounds of the machine's mammoth feet were out of earshot, the five crossed the street and entered the next stretch of alley. The air still burned Simon's nostrils, and he had to fight to keep from coughing. Black streaks of soot lined the walls and pavement. Shards of metal and glass lay strewn about, but there was no one else in sight. The silhouette had vanished without a trace. Had he imagined it? *Who could that have been?*

"Shrapnel," Chin whispered, kicking one offending piece.

Simon swallowed. One shot of the cannon in their direction would have cut through all five of them. He pictured Charity's face, hearing that she'd lost him too.

"Aaaah!"

Pain shot through Simon's leg before he realized he was falling. He hadn't been watching, and he tripped over a stray piece of metal. His left leg buckled under the pain in his shin, and he tumbled to the ground. His right hand landed hard on a piece of glass, slicing his palm. Before he could move, Chin was there, pulling out a handkerchief and wrapping it tightly around Simon's hand.

"Thanks," Simon whispered, and he pulled himself back up. He dared not linger too long, or else the others would worry about his ability to keep going. "Who was that?" he added, hoping to deflect attention. No one gave an answer.

Simon made every effort to hide his limp and his bleeding hand. He was just about to give up, though, when Zane finally pulled to the side and motioned toward a door. It appeared to be plywood nailed over an opening, but when Zane knocked, the plywood door opened, and dim light spilled out onto the alley pavement. Simon felt a rush of relief; they were here.

Jack and Simon didn't waste time. As soon as they entered the room, they found the nearest cushions on the floor and sat down. Chin greeted the host with a hearty embrace.

"Glen, I am delighted to see you. Thank you for seeing us."

"The pleasure is mine, Chin. Please, sit. Garrett, there is a pitcher of water and some cups on the table."

In minutes, all were seated and gulping water. Simon drained his cup and was grateful when Glen came with a refilled pitcher to replenish his glass.

"Tell me," Glen asked as he sat on a chair near the door, "how was your trip?"

Simon began to choke on his water, instantly feeling embarrassed at his reaction. He looked up at his host, a tall, thin man with almost no hair. Glen looked back at Simon with a curious smile, then turned to Chin.

"It was as expected, Glen. The important point is that we are here."

"Yes, and that prompts me to my next question," Glen replied. "Why exactly *are* you here?"

Chin's face flinched for a moment, and Simon suspected that this older man may have forgotten a previous conversation. After all, why would Chin come if he had not already arranged things, at least to a certain extent?

"When we spoke last, I was visiting Centra for business. I was unable to say much to you then, but I am very glad we are able to meet now. First, I have something for you." Chin stood, and reached into an inside pocket of his jacket.

"The food you gave. That is not enough already?" Glen asked as Chin handed him a packet of papers, folded in half.

"I find this to be more valuable by far," Chin answered. "I hope it is a help to you."

Glen's eyes grew wide. "Mark, Philippians, Romans . . . How much is here, Chin?"

"Not enough, to be sure. I was able to copy only portions of what we have, but even that is not complete."

"It has been so many years," Glen said, a tear in his eye. "I haven't seen Romans in ages."

"I was wondering if, perhaps, you had other portions of the Word available."

Glen's gray eyes stared at Chin for a moment. At first, Simon thought they were in trouble, but Glen must have just been deep in thought. With a blink of an eye, he rose quickly and walked across the sparse room.

"Follow me."

Everyone rose, and Simon noticed that Zane and Garrett looked as confused as he was. Glen walked through the only open doorway and led them into a closet with a sink, an exposed heating element, and two cooking pots. His kitchen. Through the next door, they moved into a room with a cot and a toilet. A door on the other side of that room opened to a tiny closet, but Glen slid the back wall to the side and walked into darkness.

Chin followed, turning on his flashlight. Everyone else did the same. The narrow tunnel turned a sharp right immediately past the doorway, and light was nonexistent save for the beams each Messenger held in his hand. Simon mused that this would have completely unsettled him a year ago. But now, he felt right at home.

The tunnel wasn't long; it led to a room that barely accommodated the six men. The room held an eclectic collection of knickknacks: a mug with a picture of a tower on it, "Paris" written near the top; a stout, round doll made of wood and painted with intricate designs; a woven hat of many colors. Simon shone his light on each one, studying what he could without touching any of them.

Glen reached up to the highest shelf. With one finger, he tipped the spine of one book back from a row of a dozen others.

"This is a book of the Psalms. It is in our language, not Hebrew. I do not recall who translated it, but all of the psalms are included. Here—it's yours."

"Is this your only copy?" Chin asked. He was visibly moved by the gift.

Glen smiled. "I have enough of it right here." He pointed to his temple. "Take care of it. And as you are able, send us a copy of all that you have."

Chin nodded. "We will. May God help us."

"Amen," Glen responded. "Now, I imagine the dawn is not far. Stay here. Garrett and Zane can arrange for the truck to come for you at nightfall. They don't have far to go tonight."

All agreed. Zane and Garrett left, and Chin, Jack, and Simon stayed in the front room and settled on cushions for rest. Simon considered what Glen's early life might have been like, but he didn't wonder long. Sleep came quickly and carried him through the day.

"Psalm ninety-eight. 'Oh sing to the LORD a new song, for He has done marvelous things! His right hand and His holy arm have worked salvation for Him. The

Lord has made known His salvation; He has revealed His righteousness in the sight of the nations.'"

The truck rumbled down the road, so the three stowaways took advantage of the noise cover. This time around, they decided to risk easier detection for the sake of sitting in one larger space in the midst of a fort constructed by stacks of boxes. They were much farther back in the cargo space of the truck this time, thanks to the help of Garrett and Zane. The boxes did not contain food, but random goods from the stockpile Garrett had mentioned the night they met.

"Do we have that one already?" Jack asked. "It sounds familiar."

"Parts of it," Chin affirmed.

"Does it sound like our translation?" Simon wondered.

"From what I can recall. It will be interesting to compare this to what we have, maybe see if there are patterns here and there in word choice."

"So, is Centra really that bad off, Chin? I guess I figured they'd be about the same as us, or even better."

"Messengers in Centra have many factors against them. The closer you are to the central government, the more scrutiny you are under. Centra is the capital and dedicated to being the example for the rest of the country in stamping out all outside, regressive, or harmful perspectives—all perspectives but their own, in other words."

Simon remembered that Mr. Burroughs, the man who challenged him in the Arena in March, was from Centra. He now understood that Burroughs's presence there in front of his grandmother, Louise Baden-Druck, would have been a particular embarrassment because her grandson was the reason an official from Centra had come to the questioning—something she should have been able to handle. He also understood that Mr. Burroughs's failure to defeat Simon would have been a bittersweet victory for her.

"Then you have the factor of being a big city," Chin continued. "During good times, big cities have big churches. During hard times, well . . . Those who come to church merely for prestige or influence suddenly see no need to be a part of the community anymore. There's nothing to be gained. That happened to Westbend too, to some extent, long before New Morgan."

Chin closed the book and stared at his feet, his legs stretched out before him. "There's also the fact that Westbend was closer to the seminary. As a result, the Westbend culture was affected. Westbend had a reputation for a strong community of pastors."

"There must have been something else too, though," Simon cut in. "Garrett told me I don't know anything about the dangers of being a pastor." The words still stung. "What did he mean by that?"

Chin took a deep breath and let it out slowly. "After the Westbend Massacre, there was a protest in Centra. A group of pastors walked the streets in front of the Centra Arena the following week. Security surrounded them. One by one, they . . . they were killed. Beheaded. Right there, in front of the crowds." Chin's face was a rock, but it was threatening to crumble. "So many flocks without their shepherds. Any Messengers who were not already underground quickly vanished. And without their leaders . . ."

Silence filled the space. Simon wondered if Garrett had lost his own pastor that day. Or if he was related to anyone who'd been at the protest. He considered that he and Garrett might have more in common than either of them had realized.

"The more I learn about this world, the more disgusted I get with it," Jack confessed without a hint of humor.

Chin turned back a few pages in his book. "Psalm ninety-four. 'O LORD, how long shall the wicked, how long shall the wicked exult? They pour out their arrogant words; all the evildoers boast. They crush Your people, O LORD, and afflict Your heritage.'"

"'In the world you will have tribulation. But take heart; I have overcome the world.'" Jack's words were slow, solemn. Simon could tell by Jack's face that he was still stricken by Chin's story. But the Message, Simon knew, did its work. Even when none of them felt much better.

"Where is that from?" Simon asked.

"The Book of John. Jesus said it to His disciples," Chin answered for Jack.

"Well, I'd be okay if Jesus came back now and overcame everything for good."

"Amen. Come, Lord Jesus," Chin answered.

Chapter Ten

I was first. I reached the tomb first. Peter was behind me, but—of course—he was the first to go inside. The burial linens were there, and His facecloth too, folded neatly. To think He took the time to fold His facecloth! I believed right away. I didn't understand much, but I believed that Jesus is the Christ, the Son of God. To think of it! It was His plan all along! He became the least. And now, through Him, we are sons; we are His brothers.

Mary saw Jesus, and what did He say to her? "Go to My brothers and say to them, 'I am ascending to My Father and your Father, to My God and your God.'" Brothers. Puts a new perspective on things when God calls Himself your Father. Puts a new perspective on fellow believers. Puts a new perspective on my own brother.

When we saw the empty tomb and abandoned linens, Peter and I went back home. What else could we do? So we waited. We waited for Jesus with our brothers and sisters.

■ ■ ■

"Uh, Chin? Where are we?" Simon was relieved that they had been allowed to maneuver their way through the boxes during the day and even open the truck door. But the darkness that greeted them was blinding.

A beam of light snapped on as Chin's initial response. The light, however, merely shone on more boxes.

"We're in an abandoned warehouse. Occasionally, the Messengers use this space for storage."

Simon flipped his light on. "Well, if this means we don't have to spend twenty-four hours in a trailer, I'm all for it."

Jack turned on his light and hopped to the ground. "Think this place has a toilet anywhere?"

"I'm not certain it would be operational," Chin answered.

"Next guy's problem," Jack said as his beam moved away and toward a wall.

"Chin? You think Jack's okay?" Simon asked after the beam made it to and through a door.

"Why do you ask?"

"Well, he's been moody lately, and I know it has a lot to do with Micah. But I think there's more. He won't talk about his parents . . . and do you remember that stuff he was saying the other night when he was out of it? Why would he join the military?"

"Well," Chin responded, "I do know that he finished Preparatory School. Now, he must work if he wishes to remain a citizen of Westbend. And we need as many of those as possible. Increasingly, the Messengers are slipping below New Morgan's surveillance, which has its advantages. But we also need Messengers who are in the world and able to provide information when needed."

A barb of guilt jabbed Simon's side. He couldn't help in this way anymore. He thought to the times he had dismissed Charity's insistence that she remain unseen in the Arena. He had taken his citizenship for granted, and now he didn't have it to use in support of the Messengers.

"So what's that mean for Jack?"

"Well, results of the testing, as you know, indicate the three strongest possibilities for one's career. If the results lean toward Security or military at all, there is considerable pressure from the government to join. In addition, those who do choose this path usually have a steady career and can offer their families a bit of immunity when it comes to infractions."

"But if he's an agent of the government, people might see him as a traitor to the Messengers. And that's not gonna fly with Jack. Can't he choose another option?"

"He can, but I imagine his family would rather he take the military route, judging by his delirious comments. And don't forget: Ella's father works for the government too. Messengers who help the government are not all traitors."

Lucas Maxon was a different story, but Simon chose not to belabor the point. With all the suspicion surrounding Jack already, giving in to pressure to join the military could cost him his role with the Messengers.

Faint gray light filtered into the room, and Jack's shadow appeared in a dim rectangle. "There are a coupla bathroom stalls across this room," Jack informed, gesturing behind him. "And Simon, you're gonna love the office."

His curiosity piqued, Simon walked from the dark loading area of the warehouse building and into an enormous room with absolutely nothing in it. A row of windows near the ceiling supplied the only illumination for the massive space. Simon couldn't remember being in such an open, empty area in his entire life, and he had the sudden urge to run around the perimeter. Except Jack was there. And his leg wasn't reliable. And he was exhausted.

"Check this out." Jack nearly skipped toward the far wall. Simon followed slowly, using false ennui to cover his fatigue.

"What's so important about an office, Jack?" The room swallowed his voice, and Simon liked the idea that he could talk at full volume—even if he had to repeat himself once for Jack to hear.

"Come and see," Jack urged, holding his arm out toward the door in invitation.

The office was terribly plain, and he wondered what life would be like to sit here five days a week.

"I don't get it."

"Come on. You're Simon Clay, aren't you? Look around!"

Simon began to take in the room, noticing endless file cabinets, all set neatly in line. He walked over to the closest one and pulled. He laughed out loud. There, organized in individual folders, were pamphlets. Hundreds and hundreds of pamphlets. *Why Morganland Needs Your Help. New Morgan: A New Dawn. Clarity of Mind: Unity in Ideology.* There were countless titles that made Simon smirk with grim realization that he was witnessing, through propaganda, evidence of the steady shift from a free society to an oppressive tyranny.

"To think I used to search everywhere for these. This place must have been the Westbend distribution center for New Morgan's campaign to end all thinking."

"Suddenly, this place feels really creepy," Jack admitted.

"Listen to this one," Simon read. "'Let us never forget the importance of guarding against regressive influences. Books, for example, are a land mine for outmoded and outdated beliefs. If anyone speaks against the government or its educational system, be on guard! Anyone who trusts themselves or their literature more than our societal jewel of New Morgan are enemies of the state.' Sounds like something my old teacher would have written."

"Well, one thing's for sure," Jack decided. "You won't be bored waiting for nightfall."

Nightfall came, and they were ready. They were also famished; hours ago, they had finished all the rations Garrett and Zane sent their way. But nothing, not even hunger, could keep Simon from the hope of returning to the City before another night was over.

Chin led the way, Simon followed, and Jack closed in behind. Simon's only concern with this arrangement was hiding his injury from Jack. He looked up into the sky and prayed for safety. He prayed for success. And he prayed that he would see Malachi soon.

It may have been the relief of walking in the alleys of his familiar city instead of Centra, but Simon found their journey home to be quick and—relatively—painless. At the North Gate, Jael nodded to them in welcome. Simon had barely made it through the tunnel to the Room of the Twelve when he was attacked by a running jump and a fierce hug. Simon nearly fell over, and not so much because of being caught off-balance.

"Hey, Charity! Did ya miss me?" Jack's question was completely ignored.

"Thanks for not dying," Charity said after pulling away from Simon and assuming a falsely casual pose.

"I did my best." Simon was pretty sure he had paint on his back now, but he didn't care. He was trying, and failing, to wipe away a stupid grin.

"Where's my welcoming committee?" Jack protested.

"Most of the cargo we brought back was tools and scrap metal," Chin announced, ignoring Jack as well. "We'll need to go to the cellar and let Spence know he'll be getting a delivery soon."

Jack seemed to consider this task and accept it as the answer to his question. "Well, let's go then."

"I need to stick with John before his paint dries," Charity said. "See you later."

Simon decided to assume that the "you" was singular and bit his cheek against the threat of another grin.

When the three were halfway through the marketplace, Dr. Roth ran up to them, out of breath.

"Chin. Welcome back. You're needed in the Elders' room."

Simon watched Chin's face fall with concern.

"Don't worry," Simon assured. "We can talk to Spence. We'll see you later." He watched the fatigued Elder race with Dr. Roth to the far corner of the marketplace.

"Man. Some guys can't catch a break," Jack mused. Simon just nodded, saying a quick prayer for the Elders and all of Westbend's pastors. For their health, for their endurance, and for their lives.

"I'm hoooome!" Jack announced as he walked down the few stairs into the cellar.

Silence.

Simon and Jack looked over the counter and saw Ella working furiously on the Bot in front of her.

"Hellooo? Can you hear us?" Jack called as he hopped onto the counter. "Wearing earplugs or something?"

Ella stood up but still ignored them. She moved to the side of the Bot so that her back was facing them. Simon could see that her ears were red and without earplugs.

"Umm, hi. So. I was away on this huge adventure, and—"

Jack could say no more. He had no chance. Within milliseconds, Ella whirled around and was in his face, a wrench flailing with every phrase that poured out of her mouth.

"Adventure? Adventure?! You go out and risk your life and you don't even bother to tell anyone?! All this time, I think you actually *care* about my opinions and—feelings. And you just go off to Centra—*Centra!*—without telling a soul. At least Simon had the good sense to tell Charity so I was able to find out through some hand-me-down news. Is that all I get? Do me a favor, Jack. Could you find just five seconds out of your important life to tell me the next time you decide to go out and almost *die*? Is that too much to ask?!"

Ella was bright red from her neck to her hairline, and Simon couldn't help but chuckle. Jack's wide eyes betrayed shock and, gradually, relief.

"So, you're saying you don't want me to die? You wouldn't be thrilled if I just disappeared? Like, you'd be sad if you never saw me again?" Jack's face grew mischievous with each new question.

"Oh, Jack Lane. You are impossible." Ella crossed her arms, the wrench safely tucked near an elbow.

Spence must have come in during the scene through the back entry. He dropped a box of parts noisily to the ground.

"When are you going to learn, Ella? Don't waste your time with guys like him."

Simon cringed as he saw Jack's posture sag instantly.

"Hey, Spence. You know what? Shut up." With that, Ella hopped onto the counter and swung her legs over the other side. Grabbing Jack's hand, she pulled him toward the stairs. "C'mon, Jack. You owe me some information."

With that, Ella led Jack out of the room.

For a moment, Spence stared after them, dumbfounded. His face was contorted by consternation, as it had been the night he glared at Jack in the chapel. It was an expression that was all too familiar to Simon.

"Can you believe her? Or you, for that matter, Simon. You of all people should know the dangers we face right now. We can't be too careful. At any minute, we could find another mole in our group, another traitor. And what then? Who will die this time?"

Simon pulled himself onto the spot of the counter Jack had occupied before being ushered away. "I hear ya. You never know who's going to all of a sudden turn on you."

"Exactly!"

"I think I'm starting to figure out the secret, though."

Spence tilted his head to one side, and he walked closer. "What do you mean?"

"One of the key signs that someone's going to turn on you. It's a pattern, I think."

Spence pulled off his knit hat and slid a stool over. He mussed his curly hair a moment before pulling his hat back on. He sat on the stool backward and used the wooden back as an armrest. Simon had his attention. He waited a moment. Like his father used to.

"See, I've been betrayed a few times now, to be honest. My uncle. Micah. Even Ben for a little while. And if you think about Judas, there's a connection with all of them."

Spence stroked his chin, trying to think of any similarities among the people listed.

"It had to do with their attitude. A sin, really. And it's one I've caught myself in just recently. The more I think about it, it was a sin I faced often about a year ago."

"Hatred?"

"I don't think it starts out that way. It's much sneakier than that. Think about it: all of these people, one way or another, thought they knew everything. They definitely thought they knew better than the person they betrayed. My uncle thought he was better than me, so he justified torturing me. Micah thought I made huge mistakes, and maybe he was right. But he let that fester until he decided that I didn't deserve to live anymore. Ben thought I was going to put his family in danger, so he wanted to stop me at whatever cost. Judas thought he knew better than Jesus how to be a king. He decided Jesus was all wrong. They all had something in common: self-righteousness."

"Simon, that doesn't make sense."

"Sure it does. As soon as you think you're better than someone else, you don't have to forgive them. As soon as you think they're an unforgiveable problem, you can—maybe even should—do whatever it takes to get them out of the way or stop them from bothering you. And as soon as you believe you have nothing to repent of, you've let down your guard. The devil can take that foothold and slowly, slyly, convince you that anything is okay if you do it for the right reason—even if that reason is getting rid of someone you should be caring for."

Spence was silent. Simon wondered if Spence was following where this conversation would lead.

"I have to admit, Spence, I think you're right. I do think there's a danger of another Micah among us. But it's not coming from Jack right now." Simon waited, gauging if he dared speak the next words. "It's coming from you."

Spence stared at Simon, and Simon could feel the heat of his anger from several feet away. Scared to budge, Simon mentally prepared himself to jump behind the counter before escaping the room. If this didn't work, there was no telling where Spence's fury would lead.

"I care about you, Spence. You're my brother. So is Jack. And I get that he can be annoying, pretentious, rude, and maybe even selfish. But every time I think I'm better than him, I'm just as bad, if not worse. I forgive him. He forgives me. And Spence, I know he'd forgive you for being so hard on him after Micah's death."

"Simon?"

"Yeah?"

"Don't. Don't you ever call me Micah again." Spence's face was twisted—with anger, but with other emotions too. His jaw trembled.

Simon watched the battle play across his friend's face.

"But you might have a point," Spence conceded. "I'm not sure. I have to think about it. But you might have just saved me . . . saved me from myself."

Chapter Eleven

"Simon. It's October. You've waited four months."

"They probably don't mind. They've waited longer before."

"Simon! They are your grandparents! How can you possibly wait so long to respond to them?! After you send them an email and they hear from you for the first time in your life, you just disappear?"

"They haven't written back either, right?"

"You know that's no excuse, Simon Clay. They probably think it was a trick or something! Or that you've been killed. Or that you were caught because of the email. Who knows what they're imagining right now!"

Ella and Spence were inspecting their completed Bot, especially their new paint job. Ella, however, couldn't allow a Saturday to pass without her typical rant.

"What am I supposed to tell them, Ella? Dear Grams and Pops, Glad to know you exist. Say, that son of yours? He's dead. Your daughter-in-law too, but you probably knew that. Me? Well, I'm living underground—literally—so my other grandma isn't able to kill me for illegally worshiping God. Hope all's well with you. Hugs and kisses, Simon."

Ella rolled her eyes. "Just try, okay? Sit down and write something."

Simon rolled his eyes in turn. "Fine. I'll try."

"Really this time."

"Ella!"

"This paint really is remarkable," Spence interrupted. "Tell me again how you found it, Jack."

"Wish I could tell you. Aside from being stowed away right next to it for a few hours, I only know that it came from some Messengers in Centra. Garrett and Zane. No idea how they got their hands on it."

Simon and Spence had never talked about Micah again. But things had improved between Jack and Spence in recent weeks. The conversations were still a little strained, and Jack was a bit too polite to seem at ease, but it was progress. At least Simon hoped it was.

"Looks sharp. I mean, really. It almost looks like a piece of black paper or something," Simon commented.

The paint must have belonged to the government at some point. Simon had never seen anything quite so dark or so flat that it obscured the angles of the Bot. Even under the lights of the workshop, any hint of shape was almost impossible to see.

"It should be perfect for stealth, which is the objective for this Bot," Spence explained. "It almost has no weaponry. Too heavy. This machine has one use: to get you somewhere and back without getting caught."

"If it keeps me out of the back of delivery trucks, I'm all for it," Jack asserted.

"Well, not for long. That's the thing," Ella cautioned. "You can only go about an hour away and back without needing to recharge. This Bot runs on battery power, and you're not going to find places to charge it randomly along the roadsides of New Morgan. We're going to have to limit ourselves to short trips until we can figure out a better plan."

"Whoa. That is some Bot." Simon jerked his head quickly to see Charity descend the steps into the cellar. "What color *is* that?"

"Honestly, we don't know," Spence admitted. "But it's pretty impressive."

"Is it time, Charity?" Ella asked.

"Just about." Charity stretched her arms overhead. "I needed a break, so I thought I'd stop over now."

When Charity lifted her arms, her sleeves fell, revealing a dark reminder of her past. Simon would never get used to seeing the brand that marked her as a New Morgan slave. He noticed, however, that she continued her recent practice of altering her scar on days she painted. Now that her X-marked star brand had a new scar running down the middle, Charity would take a color she used that day to make a semicircle at the end of the scar, creating a P. The end result was that the star brand was now covered with a Chi-Rho—similar to the one in the South Gate tunnel. Simon had since learned that the

Chi-Rho was a symbol for Christ, created by some of the first Messengers using Greek letters.

The first time Simon noticed it, Charity had smiled and said, "'If the Son sets you free, you will be free indeed.' John, chapter eight."

"I'm just glad it's art," he had said, kissing her forearm. "I can't handle any more scars."

He had later looked up the chapter in the marketplace tent and studied Jesus' words.

"If you abide in My word, you are truly My disciples, and you will know the truth, and the truth will set you free." He saw that someone had written λόγος near "word" in the passage. He was thankful for the disciple who painted disciples. And he was definitely thankful for the λόγος.

"Simon? You okay?"

Embarrassed at being caught musing, Simon turned to Charity, whose arms and sleeves were back to her sides.

"Yep. Sorry. So, we ready to go?"

Ella and Spence took the cue and washed up in a work sink behind the Bot so they all could make their way to the chapel.

"'With my voice I cry out to the LORD; with my voice I plead for mercy to the LORD,'" Cyril read boldly. "'I pour out my complaint before Him; I tell my trouble before Him. When my spirit faints within me, You know my way! In the path where I walk they have hidden a trap for me.'"

"I feel like this psalm could be my theme," Simon whispered to Charity. She ignored him, gesturing for him to focus.

"'Look to the right and see: there is none who takes notice of me . . .'"

Simon nudged Charity, who continued to ignore him.

"'. . . no refuge remains to me; no one cares for my soul. I cry to You, O Lord; I say, "You are my refuge, my portion in the land of the living." Attend to my cry, for I am brought very low! Deliver me from my persecutors, for they are too strong for me!'"

Simon listened closely; this *was* his theme psalm.

"'Bring me out of prison, that I may give thanks to Your name! The righteous will surround me, for You will deal bountifully with me.' Psalm one hundred forty-two."

Simon liked listening to psalms, in part because he was thankful to have been a part of the mission that brought the entire Book of Psalms to the people of Westbend. But he also appreciated the raw honesty behind them, as if he were listening in on someone else's prayer and making it his own. He wondered about the one who wrote the psalm. What kind of trouble was he in? Did he ever get out of it?

At the end of the service, Simon was glad when Dr. Pharen sat next to him to say hello. Most of his friends chatted nearby.

"How are you feeling, Simon?" There was something earnest in his face that prevented Simon from hiding anything.

"Well, Dr. Pharen. I have to be honest. My shin still hurts from time to time, especially if I'm running. I'm worried . . ." Simon wasn't sure why he was being so candid. "Do you think I'll always be like this? Carriers have to move around, after all."

Dr. Pharen put on a pair of glasses and leaned over. "Let's take a look."

Simon instantly regretted saying anything; he knew Jack or Charity would notice and wonder what was wrong. Dr. Pharen was brief, however, feeling his shin bone and pressing at a few points. At one spot, Simon winced and inhaled to keep from adding a yelp to the surrounding conversations.

"Hmmm, I see what you mean," Dr. Pharen said with concern. "It should heal over time, but I'm afraid you have a deep tissue bruise very near your bone. You'll experience pain for quite a while. I'm hoping it isn't a fracture or a bone chip. If it is, it's a small one. But unless I can get you to the clinic . . ."

"Don't worry about it, Dr. Pharen. I'll be okay. Thank you for checking." Simon moved his leg under the pew, hoping he didn't gain any unwanted attention from anyone nearby.

"When I asked you how you were feeling, though, I didn't even think to ask about your leg," Dr. Pharen admitted.

"Oh? Oh. Thanks. I'm okay."

"Simon, I can't imagine. You've lost so much . . ."

No, this was not what Simon wanted. He knew Dr. Pharen wanted to help, but . . .

"Simon, I want to tell you something. I'm sorry."

"What?" This was unexpected.

"I'm so sorry. I wish I could have saved your father. I wanted to save him, but . . ." Simon watched as the man, clearly distressed, shook his head and looked toward the altar.

"Oh, Dr. Pharen. Please don't blame yourself," Simon began. But the memories flooded back. *Why wouldn't he blame himself?* Simon shuddered when he remembered how he had lashed out at Dr. Pharen. He had accused him of being wrong about Charity and being apathetic toward his dad.

"Ooooh, Dr. Pharen. No. I should be the one to apologize. I didn't even think about what I said. I hope you haven't worried . . ." Simon stopped again. Of course Dr. Pharen had been worrying. It suddenly occurred to Simon that Dr. Pharen's anxiety might be the reason why his health seemed to be deteriorating. In the panic of that terrible night, Simon heaped the guilt of a death on Dr. Pharen and had completely forgotten about it.

"Simon, in all my life, I never wanted to save someone more than Charity and Jonathan. I failed saving either. Charity must have been some sort of miracle, and Jonathan . . ." Dr. Pharen's voice broke.

". . . was not your fault," Simon finished. "It wasn't fair of me to say those things to you. I wasn't thinking, and I wasn't fair. Please forgive me."

By now, attention was definitely on Simon and Dr. Pharen, but it didn't matter.

"Of course, Simon," Dr. Pharen replied. "I forgive you. Could you possibly forgive me?"

"There is nothing to forgive," Simon began, but he saw pain in Dr. Pharen's face and knew that those words would not work. "Yes. Of course. I forgive you, Dr. Pharen."

Simon didn't know what to do next. Hugging him seemed awkward, but sitting there was uncomfortable too. He just sat there.

Ben must have had enough of their conversation too, because he walked over and kneeled on the pew in front of them, facing them both.

"Hey, Simon!" Ben interjected, acting oblivious to his father wiping away a few stray tears. "I just told the others too. What a job you all did last night!"

"Uh, Ben? What are you talking about?"

"Oh, sure. That's what they all said too. But I know better. It was at every single school. Genius! Divide and conquer, eh?"

"What?"

"Must've taken a lot of chalk—er, pastels, or whatever it is you use."

"Ben! What are you talking about?!"

"The messages, of course!"

Simon sighed. "Ben. What message?"

Ben reciprocated the frustration. "The messages you all posted in front of every school yesterday morning! The whole city is talking about them. You know me, I'd rather you just leave well enough alone, but . . . Well. You know. I'm getting used to it. And you're practically famous!"

"Ben. We left no messages out last night. None of us did. We haven't done that since the night . . ." *Since the night Micah died.*

"Whatever, Simon," Ben said, not believing him. "Someone did."

Simon wondered at the news. Was the movement growing? Were there more Messengers the City didn't know about rallying behind the effort to share the Word?

"What did the messages say?"

"They were all the same. I wrote it down. Hang on." Ben reached into his pocket and pulled out his wooden box of cards, a birthday gift from Simon. He slid the hidden panel of the box and exposed a message.

"Okay, here it is: 'Moving forward together is the only way to move.' Sharadona 13:1."

"Ben. That's not the Word. That's not even a book of the Bible."

Ben stared at Simon and suddenly scowled. "Well, how do you know?! You don't know all the books there are."

"Sure, Zeke taught them to me. We don't have them all anymore, but I know what they are."

"Oh, sure, Simon. Just tell me how dumb I am again. You're just so much smarter than me. And braver. And—"

"Ben," Dr. Pharen interrupted. "Your mother will be worried about us. Let's head back before daybreak."

Ben's face flushed, and he pursed his lips. Simon could tell Ben was holding back words, and Simon was glad he didn't have to hear them.

"Fine" was all Ben allowed before he stalked to the back of the chapel.

Dr. Pharen groaned as he pulled himself to a standing position. He took his cane and followed Ben. "Good night, Simon. And thank you."

Simon wanted to protest, but he just nodded. His head was too filled with questions to process anything more that night. There was a new mystery to solve, and Simon had no idea where to begin.

Chapter Twelve

Simon stared at the wall next to his bed. The bricks and mortar formed an endless labyrinth, and his finger traced a meandering path in the narrow grooves. What was he doing here? The past month had given him a renewed sense of excitement as, psalm by psalm, Dr. Roth and those in the Translation Room verified the Message. Carriers, including Jack and Simon, received missions to gradually take the vials of new Scripture to the five Archives in the city of Westbend. Those missions, in part, were why Simon felt sore, but the activity was a great distraction from all that Simon was still healing from.

But tonight was a hard hit.

Simon had been wondering why Dr. Pharen seemed to be aging right in front of his eyes, and he now knew that he, Simon, deserved part of the blame. He wasn't the only one who had suffered the night of his father's death. Others mourned too. And in his wild grief, there were few in Simon's path who were left unscathed from being in his presence.

Words didn't come, but Simon's spirit cried out to his Lord in sorrow. In repentance. In pain. His head throbbed, his leg ached, and his heart clenched in pain for Dr. Pharen, for Malachi, for his father . . . A slow fog began to encroach on the edges of his awareness, and he feared he would be too weak to push away its numbing haze.

The knock was so light, he wasn't sure he heard it at first. At the second knock, he mumbled a "Come in."

"Simon?" Charity's voice was sweet and low, and Simon felt the fog retreat just a fraction. "Simon, are you okay?"

"Charity, I don't know if I'll ever be okay," Simon said to the wall. "I wouldn't blame you if you just left me alone. I'm too broken."

He knew that most days Charity was both willing and able to rouse him out of his melancholy with a healthy dose of no-nonsense sarcasm, and he was half expecting to receive a scolding. It didn't come.

"Want to go for a walk?"

Simon didn't. He didn't want to move at all.

"Maybe just a short one?" she coaxed.

Simon groaned with more emphasis than necessary, but he pushed himself off the bed and limped across the room. He made no effort to hide his pain. The two walked down the hallway to a handful of stairs that eventually led toward the hub of the City. Simon gave up before trying to walk further and sat on the top step. Charity joined him, resting her folded hands on her knees.

"Why do people bother with me, Charity? I'm a mess."

Charity didn't respond.

"This whole time, I had no idea that Dr. Pharen felt responsible for my dad's death. What does that do to a person?! All because of something I said."

Simon held his head in his hands and waited for a reply. Nothing.

"And Malachi. Charity, I told him that I hated him. I told him that I never wanted to see him again. That's why we haven't seen him around; it's all my fault. And I want to apologize. I've prayed for a chance to see him again. But he hasn't come. Of course he hasn't. I don't deserve to talk to him anymore. I'm getting what I asked for, but everyone else is suffering too."

He looked over at Charity, who stared ahead, not moving. He suddenly felt angry toward her for ignoring him. He was overcome with the irresistible urge to shake her from her silence.

"Tell me why I'm here," he demanded.

Charity glanced over at him briefly. "Out of bed?"

"Right, why bother? Why am I in the City too, for that matter? Who gives a rip if I'm alive at all?!"

Charity looked directly at him with a look that was simultaneously tender and annoyed.

"You're here because you need to get out of your own head."

"Is that supposed to be comforting?"

"And you need to remember how many people care about you."

"By not leaving me alone?"

"Is that what you want?" Charity's eyes flashed with a challenge.

"Wait, what?"

"Were you better off in your room by yourself?"

"Well, no one was arguing with me."

"I doubt that."

Simon glared at Charity, but he was speechless. *How does she know so much?* He felt his temper rising, and he made no attempt to keep it under control.

"So now you hate me too . . ." Simon knew it was the dumbest thing he could say, but Charity was unflappable, and it was maddening.

Charity's reaction was not what he expected at all. She tossed her head back and laughed.

"Are you done being ridiculous?" she asked.

It was Simon's turn to be silent.

"Malachi doesn't hate you any more than I do. Same with Dr. Pharen. And no matter how many times you push us away, we're all going to be right here, whether you like it or not. It's how God is, and it's how we are to one another."

"Malachi isn't here."

"That's what you think."

Simon had no idea what she meant by that, but it was no use arguing. He was too frustrated to keep fighting back.

"You made mistakes, Simon. Fair enough. But you were also grieving. People know that. They're grieving too. You're not the only one who loved Jonathan. And you're also not the only reason why Malachi is gone or Dr. Pharen is sad or . . . anything else for that matter."

"You know how to make a guy feel better, don't ya?"

Charity rolled her eyes and kept going.

"Every move you make won't alter the universe. You can't take credit or blame for everything that happens. I happen to think an awful lot of you, if you haven't noticed." She paused for a moment, and Simon wasn't sure if he should allow the small smile that threatened to show. "But you have to stop thinking that the weight of the world is on your shoulders. That job's already taken, and I don't suggest you offer to replace Him."

Simon leaned his head on the wall. After a moment, Charity leaned her head on his shoulder. The two sat together in silence, contemplating each other's words. Charity had been brutally honest, but even in the harsh words, there was genuine concern. And there was truth.

"You know what? You're acting like Zeke," Simon commented.

Charity's head shook as she laughed gently. "Well, that's not so bad. I'm a fan."

"Charity?"

"Hmmm?"

Simon was hesitant to change the subject, but a mystery lurked in the back of his mind.

"Those messages in Westbend. We have an imitator."

"Mmmhmm."

"And who knows what they'll post next?"

Simon felt Charity nod.

"What are we going to do?"

Charity sighed and straightened up. Simon looked at her as she looked out into the dark tunnel ahead.

"I have no idea."

"This is not the first," Chin admitted.

Jack, Charity, and Simon were sitting with Zeke and Chin in the courtyard. It was Sunday afternoon, and a deck of cards lay ignored in the center of their table.

"Remember the night we returned from Centra?" Chin asked. "Two Carriers found a message, and they were able to erase it before dawn."

"This time," Zeke added, "we didn't catch the messages—any of them. And there would have been too many to erase anyway."

"Who's doing it?" Simon asked. Chin and Zeke both shrugged.

"We have no idea," Zeke sighed.

"The message is nonsense," Chin declared. "Vague enough to mean nothing at all. It doesn't make sense that the government is doing it; it looks like they have no control, and their message would have been bolder."

"Then who? Other citizens? What's their motivation to risk getting caught?"

Simon thought back to school cafeteria conversations he overheard when his messages first appeared. "Maybe they want an excuse to get out of school?"

"Would they risk their lives for that?!" Chin asked. "And why Saturday morning then?"

"Maybe they just want attention," Jack suggested.

"One thing's for sure," Charity mused, "there has to be more than one person involved to write in so many places at once."

"Quite right," Zeke agreed. "Whether this is a carefully planned maneuver or a ridiculous prank, we have no idea. But the most important question remains. What is there to do about it? For the sake of our fellow citizens, what course of action should we take?"

Silence took over the group, and the hum of the subdued marketplace replaced any conversation.

"It could be a trap," Jack admitted.

They all nodded.

"It might just help the other group gain momentum," Simon offered.

Agreement spread around the table.

"It could be the answer to a plea for conversation," Chin suggested.

Everyone considered the possibility.

"It definitely would be an opportunity to share the Message," Charity added.

It was decided.

Chapter Thirteen

He stared at the door. He hated this place. Months ago, to be in the room on the other side of this door meant to be a part of something powerful. To be a part of the solution to delusions and outdated ideologies. Now? Now. Now the power was slowly slipping away, and he could see it happening. What he couldn't decide yet was whether he cared enough to do anything about it.

"I know you're there," a voice called from inside the room. "Don't even bother knocking. Just come in already."

He clenched his jaw and turned the knob.

As usual, she was seated at the far end of the dark room. As usual, she had two hapless cronies standing guard in the corners. To think of the miserable hours of their days! He almost pitied them.

"You look terrible, Roderick," Louise Baden-Druck clipped. "It's beyond me how one can look so defeated." After a silent scowl and a beleaguered sigh, she continued, "And what do you have to report?"

"The messages were seen; the youth witnessed it on their way to the Arena. We had to wash everything away, as we did for the others. But there is no doubt word will spread when the adults return to work on Monday."

"The message was moronic," she lamented.

"We did not give them any message. This was what they came up with."

"Youth today are idiots."

"Isn't that our goal?"

"Silence! You're giving me a headache," Mrs. Baden-Druck hissed. "Tell me again whom we hired."

"Recent graduates from Druck-Baden Manor Life Preparation Year. A few of my more promising projects," Roderick answered with a slim but satisfied smile.

"That explains it then. Enough," she waved him away. "You're boring me. You may leave."

"Ah, there is one more thing," he mentioned.

"What now?"

"The proposal—"

"Roderick! Must I tell you again how asinine your idea is?! What could possibly make you believe it would work? It's just another waste of time. You know as well as I do that the Revemondians refuse to acknowledge our claim to the land west of the mountains. New Morgan is fortifying its troops for a full offensive campaign. The longer we let this pestilence thrive under our feet, the more distractions we have from New Morgan's realization as a world power. And you want to take a field trip—for what? Now, get out before I tell my guards to throw you out."

"That won't be necessary," Roderick Druck said, eyeing the two scrawny pawns who were no threat to him.

"One more thing, Roderick," his mother said as he turned toward the door. "Remember my promise. It's either you or the boy, and it's October now. You have eight more months."

Roderick closed the door behind him and walked away.

"So, who is this?" Simon looked up at the painted face of a kindly older man. Charity carefully added the finishing touches to his hands, which were held out, as if to offer a fatherly embrace.

"John."

"Looks like a nice guy."

"Thanks. He was, eventually. Pretty quarrelsome in his early years—with his brother, at least."

"Everyone ready?"

Cyril walked in, and a small crowd followed him from the marketplace.

"Tonight, we pair up so that each youth is with an adult," he explained. "Zeke, you're with Charity."

Simon fought back a pang of jealousy; a mission with Zeke would be something to remember. But Zeke had rescued Charity long ago, and Simon was glad to know that Charity was in good hands.

"Chin, you'll be with Jack."

"Chin! Who knew you were so young?" Jack teased, but Simon could sense a bit of annoyance that he was called a youth.

"I will go with Spence," Cyril said. Simon noticed the same reaction in their brilliant friend, and he had a hunch that Jack was feeling a bit better with the situation.

"And I will accompany Ella," Johann said from the back of the group.

"Uh, I don't want to complain," Simon started, "but this whole idea started with me months ago. I'd like to be a part of it . . . So, who am I going with?"

"Me."

A deep voice behind Simon caused him to shout in surprise, prompting the Room of the Twelve to fill with laughter. Simon whirled around to see a face he could not believe was there.

"Malachi!" Simon had no idea what to do. Or what to say. Especially since eight other people were watching. "Where've you been?! It's been four months since you were around." Simon tried to keep it light, but telltale tones of accusation edged into his voice.

"Uh, Simon? You're kidding, right?" Jack asked. "You know he drove that truck from Centra, right?"

Simon suddenly realized why the voice of the truck driver had seemed familiar. Why hadn't he recognized it?

"And he was the one who loaded the truck the night before our trip," Chin added.

"I'm willing to bet," Jack said, "that he was the one in the streets the night we visited Glen too."

Simon was frantically trying to wrap his head around all of this information, but Malachi was standing right there in front of him, and that alone was difficult to process.

"Well, are we ready to go now?" Cyril asked. Everyone else agreed, and the caravan made its way through the North Gate. Simon was only capable of putting one foot in front of the other.

"Be safe," Charity whispered.

Simon nodded. "You too."

Two by two, Michael let the Messengers out into the night. He gave Malachi a hearty slap on the shoulder as they passed through the doorway out of the City.

Simon realized he wasn't certain where exactly they were going, so he followed Malachi, wondering which direction they would head next. "Follow the stars . . ." Simon realized he had completely failed to take this Messenger's advice, despite his best intentions early in the summer to study the skies as an ever-present map. He needed a tutor.

Malachi moved quickly, but his steps were calm and confident. Simon felt his typical fear melt away as they worked silently through the maze of the city alleys. Just as he was beginning to feel safe . . .

Grrrrrrrrrrrrrrrrr.

The growl of a motor and the flash of a spotlight approached from the street ahead of them.

"Get behind me," Malachi instructed evenly.

Simon wordlessly obeyed as the two moved to the side of the alley. Simon faced away from the oncoming bot, and he watched as light flooded the alley. Simon was hidden in Malachi's shadow, but he knew they would both be caught if Malachi were spotted.

Tick tock. Tick tock.

Simon heard the ubiquitous report of a corner clock. To think the clocks used to be the greatest threat in Simon's life. Now, they were merely a backdrop to greater horrors. Such as a Bot hunting you down for sport in the middle of the night.

The light revealed the details of the alley in garish tones. Broken glass glittered on the pavement. Refuse containers overflowed with rubbish from residents who still had homes and families and empty cans from legitimate rations. Simon felt nostalgic for the days when he only suspected that there was more than meets the eye in New Morgan. Now he knew the truth, and much of it he wished he could forget. *The truth will set you free . . .* And then there was Charity. Charity had seen more than he had, and yet she rejoiced in the truth. The λόγος. The Message.

The light and grumble of the Bot faded away, and nothing happened. Simon marveled that he had not been more terrified. Capture seemed imminent, but how many other times was this the case? He was no longer surprised by the battles, the struggles, the setbacks. He was only weary of them.

Malachi tapped Simon, and they moved forward. Two blocks later, Malachi stopped.

"This is the place."

Simon knew it well. They were standing directly in front of the Westbend West Sector library. He chuckled.

"But Malachi, no one comes here."

It wasn't up for debate, of course, and Simon knelt to the pavement and began. Malachi stood watch, only feet away from Simon, who was crouched in the middle of the street, working as quickly as he could with the pastel Charity had given him earlier. Before long, he stood and looked at his handiwork.

IF YOU ABIDE IN MY WORD, YOU ARE TRULY MY DISCIPLES, AND YOU WILL KNOW THE TRUTH, AND THE TRUTH WILL SET YOU FREE.

JOHN 8

Malachi nodded and led Simon back into the darkness.

Simon felt accomplished and walked with a level of satisfaction. But the mission tonight was far from over.

"Malachi?" Simon began, talking quietly. "I didn't mean what I said. That night."

"Yes. You did."

A lump formed in Simon's throat at the truth. He knew that *hate* was not a word you used with anyone. He had learned from his father long ago that hatred should be reserved solely for Satan and his demons, who had no good in them and no hope for redemption. "People aren't the enemy, Simon. They're the prize." Simon's memory rang with his father's words, and they accused him with a lack of trust and forgiveness. His own words had been a mockery of Jonathan's last words: "Simon, forgive them." More than that, Malachi needed no forgiveness. He had done nothing wrong.

"Malachi? I'm sorry. I'm so sorry."

They were walking side by side, as they did the time Malachi rescued Simon from Security when he had been separated from Micah. Simon wondered just how far back Micah had been tempted to go astray. But what mattered now were his own grave mistakes.

Malachi stopped for a moment and placed his hands on Simon's shoulders. Eye-to-eye, Malachi responded, "You are forgiven."

There was nothing Simon could do to keep the tears from falling down his face in an instant flood of sorrow and relief. Mercifully, Malachi gave him a firm, reassuring embrace and turned them both back forward on their journey.

"I miss him, Malachi."

"I know you do."

"Why did he have to go so soon?"

"That is not for either of us to say. You know that."

"Is he okay?"

"You know the answer to that as well. He is with the Lord. He is in the Lord's presence. What could be better?"

Simon smiled. "You know the answer to that, Malachi. The Last Day. The day we are waiting for."

Malachi tilted his head back and laughed loudly, fearlessly, as if death and hell were no match for the war at hand.

Simon realized they were nearing Merchant Street. Simon's first instinct was to dart away to another direction, but he knew already that Malachi would insist they press on. As they walked closer, he noticed that they were walking along the east side of the Pharens' apartment building. He was looking directly across the street at 2350 Merchant Street. The home that had kept him safe for years. To think that he spent some of those years bored and discontent, yearning to break free from its walls into a world that held adventure and excitement. And yet, he realized as he looked at the dark windows, this was no longer home. There was no one within those walls who loved him. But he did have a home filled with countless brothers and sisters in Christ who loved him dearly, who loved him enough to stand by him during dark times. Who loved him enough to bear with him when he was extremely unlovable. Who loved him enough to tell him when he was wrong.

They crossed the street, and Simon approached the alley that once had been busy with Messengers moving in and out of his father's workshop. To his right, the square black door he had exited for countless assignments now stood silent and shut. He reached out and laid his hand against the cool metal. Without thinking, he knocked on it, half expecting it to open to a bright square of light and the smiling face of his dad.

Nothing. Simon sighed, but he somehow felt better. He looked up at Malachi and nodded. There was no doubt that this had been part of Malachi's plan, and it worked. He could say good-bye to this place and to this chapter of life with peace. He was ready to go home.

"I'm glad you came back, Malachi," Simon said as they walked behind the building and over the tunnel that by now was likely filled back in. "But are you going to leave again?"

"I will always be around when you need me, whether you know it or not."

Simon chuckled at the classic Malachi answer.

Malachi led him through twists and turns that Simon thought he should know by now, but he was hopelessly lost. At last, they reached the South Gate, where Jael's eyes peeked through the small slide window upon their arrival. Jael opened the door, and Simon turned around to thank Malachi for . . . well, for so many things. But Malachi was already gone.

Chapter Fourteen

"You're safe!"

It wasn't until he heard those two words that he realized he hadn't been using the South Gate often enough lately.

Mrs. Meyer's beaming smile and tight hug confirmed that he had been in withdrawal of some much-needed mothering.

"Now, look at you. You are a sight, let me tell you. Have you been eating nothing these days? Look at these cheeks. And these arms! My. I won't be surprised if I hugged you again and felt nothing but ribs underneath your jacket. What is *wrong* with you, Simon Clay? Don't you know you can get food from Mrs. Meyer when you need it?!"

Simon allowed himself to be led toward Martha Meyer's bakery booth, and he didn't resist when she loaded his arms full of bread, rolls, and treats.

"Now, don't you dare come back around here with no more than skin on your bones—" she stopped herself there and then clarified, "But don't you dare make me wait so long for a visit, you hear?"

Simon was still reeling from the night's mission, but he was present enough to know better than to contradict Mrs. Meyer. He'd seen her at worship every week, but during those times especially, she seemed withdrawn and melancholy. He'd assumed she wanted her space, but he realized now that leaving her alone might have been a huge mistake.

"How are you, Mrs. Meyer?" Simon's emphasis hinted that he was asking more than small talk, and a shadow passed over her face.

"Some days are hard, you know," she answered, and her tone confided that she realized he really did know. "But the Lord is good, and my George is with Him."

"Amen," Simon affirmed. "Say, Mrs. Meyer, would you like to sit with me during church this weekend?"

Mrs. Meyer's face lit up, and her eyes were shining. "It would be a joy and an honor, Simon Jonathan Clay."

He was still smiling when he came to the Room of the Twelve, but the people in the room were not as jovial.

Charity ran across the entire length of the room when Simon entered and threw her arms around him, but there was no cheerfulness in her greeting.

"I'm so glad you're safe."

"Yes, I'm safe. Why?"

"You took so long."

"Ah. Well, Malachi took a detour on the way home." Simon decided not to elaborate at the moment.

"Malachi. Is Malachi okay?"

"Yes, of course. He came with me to the South Gate before leaving. Charity, what's wrong?"

"Some of us heard terrible sounds, like a battle, but we had no idea where it was coming from. And not all of us are back yet."

"It's okay. Malachi and I are back. We're all safe now," Simon tried to soothe.

"No, Simon. Not all of us are back yet, even now."

"What? Who are we missing?"

Charity bit her bottom lip before softly saying, "Spence and Cyril."

Simon's heart plummeted. They had gone out together, of course. So if they were both missing, there would be no way of knowing . . .

"Let's not fear the worst," Johann cautioned. "Simon only just arrived. And it appears he had been detained by Mrs. Meyer," he added, eyeing the baked bounty that was now lying at Simon's feet after Charity's fierce embrace. "Countless factors could be keeping them. Even so, let us pray for their safety."

An hour passed, and still no news came. Those living in the City were sent to bed, and those who lived elsewhere were accompanied home by escorts. There was discussion over whether Ella could spend the night in the City, but the next day was a school day, and her absence could bring suspicion. Only Zeke and Johann stayed up, waiting for reports that all others were home safe and holding out hope that Spence and Cyril would arrive.

"Simon, I'm worried," Charity said as he walked with her to her room.

"I am too."

"What happens if they're caught?"

Simon didn't need to answer. They both had experienced captivity under New Morgan's government.

"Simon?" Charity asked as they reached her door. "What are we doing? The Messengers, I mean. It feels like every day is a battle against the whole world—more than the world. Heaven and earth."

Simon knew exactly how she felt. And Zeke had said as much during his dad's funeral as well.

"Is it even worth it?" she continued. "Sometimes, it feels like there's no way out. Each new day, something will get harder. Something will get worse. We'll lose another battle, and we'll eventually all be gone, one by one."

Simon hated hearing Charity talk this way. It was strange; he was often the one looking bleakly into the evil of the world, and Charity was ready to bring him out of whatever cloud threatened him. But he couldn't forget that she had her fair share of fears too, and it was his duty, his privilege, to return the support.

"If God weren't on our side, I would have stopped fighting a long time ago. But who knows how many more battles there would be if He weren't preserving us? And we've seen a success or two along the way."

He hadn't realized until he spoke the words, but he was holding her hand. He sat down on the floor with his back against the door and tugged until she joined him.

"One thing I know for sure. We have a Message, and it's worth dying for. My parents believed it. And they're not the only ones. I believe it. You believe it."

Simon paused and let the silence work its power in calming them both. He knew these were the kinds of things his dad would say to him. They were the kinds of things Charity often said to him too. He took a breath and continued slowly. "Century after century, believers have died rather than turn away from their Savior. Century after century, believers have seen battles rage—many that seemed like total losses. But the battles pale in comparison when we remember that Jesus has already won. He's won the war, and Satan can never change that."

"'If God is for us, who can be against us?'" Charity recited. Simon could tell she was more at peace.

"'Weeping may tarry for the night, but joy comes with the morning.' Good night, Charity." Simon kissed her and helped her to her feet before leaving her for the night.

Chapter Fifteen

He was the first one. The first of us Twelve to lose his life for the Way.

Can it be? I can't believe he's gone! My brother James killed for a political stunt. To think I wanted to get away from him so often. To think we spent so much of our time together fighting. Sons of Thunder, they called us. Oh, what a fool I was. What am I to do now?

Who are my brothers? I remember when Jesus asked those very words. His own brothers didn't believe in Him at the time. "Who are My mother and My brothers?" And on the cross, Jesus told me that Mary was now my mother to care for. Yes, I have many brothers. These disciples are my brothers, and Jesus called Himself our Brother. Now James is with Him and our Father. I'm going to miss him until we meet again. But until then, I'll tend to my brothers and sisters here.

■ ■ ■

Simon watched Ella enter the Room of the Twelve, trying to read from her demeanor what news she had to bring. It didn't look good.

Charity noticed and climbed down the ladder. John was complete, and she was working on the outline of the penultimate disciple.

"Ella? What's the news?" Simon wanted his voice to sound light, but he knew he failed. It didn't matter; Ella's expression immediately crumbled into a sob. Charity ushered Ella to sit down, and they all sat at the feet of the newest project.

"The messages were found, and of course everyone is talking about them. That's the good part. Most of them assume that they came from the same people who left the last two messages, but not everyone agrees. At least, that's what I could tell from listening in the hallways and cafeteria."

Simon smiled. He remembered the surreal feeling of eavesdropping on others to listen about his latest work.

"The teachers were horrible. Instead of class time, it was like a trial all day. Mr. Mortimer—he's our teacher this year—paced the floor all day long, just trying to get a rise out of us."

It was the first time Simon realized how much life was happening at school without him.

"How did Ben handle it?" he asked.

"His face kept changing colors all day—from red to really pale—not that I can blame him. I tried my best to look innocent, but I'm sure I failed miserably. My knees would not stop shaking!"

"Did your teacher say anything to you?" Charity asked.

"I was just sure at any minute, he was going to grab me or Ben and drag us out of the room. But then, this is the worst of it . . ." Ella swallowed, and a tear rolled down her face.

"There's this sweet kid, Sam. He's new and acts pretty nervous all the time. Well, he was acting strange all day. He's not to blame, of course, but he's one of those guys who gets uneasy a lot, you know? Well, Mr. Mortimer must have suspected him, and he calls him up to the front of the classroom and yells at him in front of everyone! He accuses him of all sorts of things, and all Sam could do was stand there and shake. I felt so terrible for him. And then, without warning, Mr. Mortimer hits him! And pulls him out of class. Oh, Simon, they'll let him go, won't they? When they find out he doesn't know anything?"

Simon and Charity were silent. Charity absently stroked the brand on her forearm. Ella whimpered.

"And then when we got home from school, a special bulletin came on the news right away. They said they caught the culprits from the Darkness who 'brought destruction and terror to our city.' They showed photos of Spence and Cyril. They both looked terrible. The reporter told everyone that Westbend Security is doing an excellent job to keep everyone safe but to report any suspicious behavior of any kind to authorities. And then . . ."

Simon didn't think he could take any more "and thens." It didn't look like Ella could either.

"They showed a sketch of you, Simon. They said you are the leader of the Darkness and you were to be caught at all costs. Everyone must immediately report it if they find you, or else they will be considered part of the Darkness too." Ella paused to wipe the tears that came freely now.

"The leader? That's generous." But Simon didn't feel very thankful for the designation. Now, the entire city, not just Security and the Bots—not just his uncle and grandmother—would be looking for him.

"One more thing," Ella managed to say. Simon's heart sank.

"They're also reporting more on the conflict with Revemond. It sounds like they're getting ready to go to war. Can you imagine? War! They're rounding up all troops and—and—recent graduates who are eligible for the military."

Simon and Charity stared at Ella, who could no longer keep it together.

"Simon, Charity, what about Jack?! He was supposed to have until December to announce his career choice, but now? They're going to hunt him down. Spence, one of my closest friends, is in prison. I can't—I can't lose Jack too!"

Ella's words ended as her sobs began. Charity reached out and held Ella close, bracing her against the attacks that she endured. Simon watched Ella's typically cheerful face turn into one of agony. *Poor Ella*. She had become an official Messenger just two months ago, but she was already learning all that came with the role.

Simon walked into Spence's cellar and immediately regretted it. The sleek, stealthy Bot sat motionless in the heart of the room, and all was dark. In fact, with the special paint treatment, Simon could see only what appeared to be a large black spot in the center of the space. No sounds of work or laughter warmed the workshop, and Simon felt as hollow as the room. He sat on the steps, wondering what was next for the Messengers. The Book of Psalms had given them purpose and more of the λόγος, but what would happen when those were all safely stored in the Archives? Spreading the Word on the streets would keep the people of Westbend mindful that there was a truth to be discovered. But with mixed messages and imminent capture, was it worth it? And what about Revemond? What about Jack?

Simon wasn't sure where he would find his friend, but he wasn't here. Simon began walking the tunnels of the City, looking for any clues to where Jack might be. In the Room of the Martyrs, he found Mrs. Meyer handing a small bag of rolls to a young woman.

"Simon! How are you, dear?"

"I've been better, Mrs. Meyer. And you?"

"Ah yes. Well, I suppose I can say the same. But it sure is good to see you!"

"I'm looking for Jack. Have you seen him yet tonight?"

"As a matter of fact, he came in through my house this evening. But I haven't seen him lately."

"That helps. Thank you, Mrs. Meyer!"

Heading into the marketplace, Simon couldn't help but feel that it was more subdued than usual, even for a Monday night. He made his way toward the tent in the middle of the room.

"Hi, Sol."

"Simon! It's been a little while, hasn't it?"

"I suppose you're right," Simon said, caught a little off guard. "I'm wondering if you've seen Jack."

"Oh, sure. He stopped by and read this passage here," Sol said, gesturing toward the album full of passages. Simon walked up to the book and read the portion Jack had been studying.

"Romans, chapter thirteen," Simon read aloud. "'Let every person be subject to the governing authorities. For there is no authority except from God, and those that exist have been instituted by God.' Ouch. That's a tough one."

"It sure is," Sol agreed. "And Paul meant it when he wrote it. But there's also this . . ."

Sol paged through the album and came to the Book of Acts.

"'But Peter and the apostles answered, "We must obey God rather than men."' Chapter five."

"Hmmm, those don't seem to go together, do they, Sol?"

Sol smiled. "Paradox. We humans hate it, but God uses it all the time. Navigating this world takes a careful balance, and the Word keeps us in check—even when it doesn't make much sense."

"This kinda makes me think about the Commandments. 'Honor your father and your mother.' That includes all authority, right?"

"Aha! Yes. A good commandment. But what happens when authority doesn't obey 'You shall have no other gods'?"

Simon understood the struggle Jack was going through. He thought about a conversation he had with his dad about the fiery furnace.

"Shadrach, Meshach, and Abednego. They went through this. They were willing to obey the king, but they were also willing to die rather than betray God."

"Excellent example. They disobeyed the law only when it disobeyed God. And even then, they were willing to obey the law's punishment rather than go against the Lord."

"Thanks, Sol. I'm going to see if I can find Jack."

Simon flipped back to Romans and copied down a passage before leaving. Sol waved as Simon left to make his way through more tunnels, trying to decide where Jack would be. Passing through the mosaic hallway and mahogany-paneled room, he looked inside the chapel. The place of worship was empty and silent. Simon felt a sense of awe but also disappointment. It just wasn't the same without the people.

As Simon left, he stared into the eyes of the stoic angel in the mosaic. Lucifer. What tricks wouldn't he pull to attack God's people? Simon shuddered; he knew the answer.

Simon was out of ideas. He began wandering through tunnels until there was no more light. Simon flipped on his flashlight as he realized what path he was taking. *Jack wouldn't have . . . would he?* Simon wanted to turn back, but if this was where Jack was . . .

The first face that greeted him was bone-white and missing a jaw. Simon suddenly felt cold, but he moved forward. Forcing himself to take step after step, he found the coffin in the corner of the room. It was no longer dusty, and a small note rested on top. Simon bent down to read it.

To live is Christ, and to die is gain.

Philippians 1:21

Jack had been here. Simon once again realized that Jonathan was not just his father. He had been important to more people than Simon would ever know. He was the kind of Postmaster who would tend your wounds in the middle of the night. He was the kind of pastor who would sing to you in your last hours. He was the kind of scholar who would risk his life to come and help translate the forbidden Message. And Jonathan wasn't the only one, Simon knew. Chin. Zeke. Cyril. They were all putting themselves last for the sake of Christ and to serve His people.

Simon was weary. Where could Jack be now? And what time was it? Simon guessed that the hours were growing close to dawn; Jack must be on his way to his home by now. He trudged back through the tunnels and made his way up the few stairs to his hallway. He didn't even pay attention to the fact that his door was slightly ajar until he pushed it open and saw a figure sitting on the trunk at the foot of his bed.

"Jack."

"Where've you been?"

Simon couldn't help but chuckle. "Following you, just not fast enough." Simon relayed his trek, starting at the cellar, and Jack nodded at each point.

"You just missed the Room of the Twelve. Except I didn't go in. Ella and Charity were there, and . . . and Ella was . . . upset. I wanted to . . . but . . . I just . . ."

Simon nodded. No explanation was needed. Simon turned on the light, causing Jack to blink in protest. Simon pulled a chair from against the wall and sat down. For a few moments, neither of them spoke.

"They're going to find me," Jack said.

"Yeah."

"Or if they don't, they'll know I'm part of the Darkness."

Simon smirked at Jack's use of the term. "Yep."

"And if they find me, I'm going to have to fight in the war against Revemond."

Simon didn't speak, but he nodded slowly.

"I never did like the military."

At this, Simon laughed. "You're already a soldier, Jack." With that, he pulled out a small sheet of paper and handed it to Jack.

"'The night is far gone; the day is at hand,'" Jack read. "'So then let us cast off the works of darkness and put on the armor of light.'"

"Romans, chapter thirteen," Simon finished. "You'll be serving two armies, Jack. One may not win—"

"Is it wrong to hope it doesn't?" Jack smirked.

". . . but the other one already has," Simon ended.

Jack looked down at the paper. "Thanks."

"Try to stay alive, all right?" Simon knew that losing Jack would be losing a brother. He didn't want to think about it. They'd all lost so many people.

"I'll do my best," Jack answered with a smile. "Hey, Simon?"

"Yeah?"

"Can I crash here tonight?"

Simon laughed. "Any time."

"Great." And without hesitation, Jack kicked off his shoes and jumped behind him into Simon's bed.

Simon begrudgingly accepted the quilt that was tossed his way and found a spot on the floor.

Chapter Sixteen

"Here."

Ella picked up the paper and rolled her eyes. "It's about time."

It was November, and Operation Distract Ella was in full swing. Charity and Simon were constantly trying to find ways of keeping Ella busy since Spence and Jack were both in the government's control, one way or the other.

One effort included Ella serving as a tutor for both Charity and Simon. She would bring homework or her textbooks and teach Ella and Simon what she had learned in school that day. Charity would lament that she was too far behind to understand much of it, but Simon was impressed with how quickly she caught up. "Besides, you're helping Ella," he reminded her one time after their class was finished. "And it's not like they're teaching anyone much. I imagine they've cut the history books into pieces before giving out anything."

This was one such instance, where the three gathered around the table with a pamphlet in the middle. Simon knew the lessons were losing their excitement for Ella, who wasn't keen to talk about the current events of failed diplomacy talks with Revemond. The piece of paper he handed to Ella was a desperate attempt to keep the distractions coming.

> Caleb and Jane,
>
> Please pardon my delay. It may become increasingly difficult to give you updates, and this one is not easy to give. Jonathan has moved farther from me and closer to Abigail. Even so, I have family. There may come a day when walls will fall and I can see you. I hope so.
>
> Joy comes in the morning,
> Simon

"It might be too risky to send at this point," Simon conceded.

Ella nodded slowly. "The email address goes to a Revemond domain, after all. But I bet my dad could help us."

"Ella, is it really worth it?"

"I'm tired of being careful, Simon. Don't you just want to be risky sometimes?"

"Ella. Do you know me? Just remember that some of my risks have led to a public trial in the Arena, a nearly fatal Bot fight, and the death of a friend."

Ella looked at Charity at the mention of the Bot fight, and she was sober by the end of the list.

"Okay. Fair points. But don't forget that the Arena trial is what opened my eyes to the Message. You know, the Message worth dying for."

Simon sighed. "Yes, but it's worth living for too."

Ella bit her lower lip and thought, looking back and forth between Simon and Charity. "I'll ask my dad and see what he thinks."

"So, Ella," Charity asked, "how's Ben?"

The room dimmed with Ella's frown. "He won't talk to me."

"Not at all?" Simon asked. They hadn't seen Dr. Pharen or Ben in weeks.

"Ever since the day when that kid, Sam, was investigated, Ben has completely ignored me."

Simon snorted. "I know how that feels."

"Do you think Ben's okay?" Charity asked.

Ella shrugged. "I have no idea."

Simon picked up the pamphlet in front of them. It was a weekly reader given to all New Morgan schools to keep students up to date with the latest government lies. REVEMOND PROVOKES WESTERN FRONT screamed on the front page of the leaflet. Simon opened it to find a cartoon with two children huddled together in a street. From the alley, a dark shadow with dozens of angry eyes seeped out, threatening to surround the helpless pair. In front of them, words were scrawled on the pavement in dripping letters: "The Darkness Is Waiting for You!" Simon folded the paper back over without comment.

"I don't know about you, but I think I've learned enough for today."

"Well, hello, Simon, how have you been?" Dr. Roth had been working for at least five minutes before she looked up and noticed him standing in the doorway of the Translation Room. Work tables around the room were covered with papers, indicating that others had been working throughout the day, but it was late now and Dr. Roth was the only one present. It was a Wednesday night, and the City was quiet.

"Hi, Dr. Roth. I guess I don't see you too often lately, since we don't have any new Messages to bring you."

"Well, that Book of Psalms gave us plenty of work! Even though it was in our language, we checked the translation against the Hebrew portions to be sure it was reliable. We're nearly finished with the project, though," she said, waving an arm toward the tables. "You'll have to think of some other places to find hidden passages," she added, smiling.

Simon smiled back, but he was already thinking about the question he was about to ask. Was he ready to hear the answer?

"Dr. Roth, you knew my dad when he was younger, right?"

"Yes, since the time he was studying at the seminary."

"So you knew my mom too?"

"Oh yes. In fact, we went to college together. Your mother was a wonderful woman, Simon." Dr. Roth's eyes shined behind her glasses, but her smile was sad. "I wish you could have known her better."

"Well, I guess that's why I'm here. I mean, I know a little about my mom from what Dad would say, but I wouldn't ask him too often. It was hard on him."

"I understand," she said. She sat down at a work table and motioned Simon toward a nearby chair. She pulled off her glasses and rested them on her head. She rubbed her eyes, and Simon realized how tired she must be. He felt a pang of guilt for keeping her.

"I could come back another time," he said. It had taken him months to work up the courage to come after Charity made the suggestion in August, but there was no sense in keeping Dr. Roth too late.

"Nonsense. Have a seat. Now," she said as Simon obeyed, "what do you want to know?"

Simon shrugged. "Anything." He had a million questions, but he'd be satisfied with whatever she could tell him. "What was she like?"

"She had this perfect blend of bravery and kindness. She didn't hold back from the truth, and she stood up to anyone who was doing wrong. Her family didn't appreciate that very much," Dr. Roth mused. "But she was so patient, especially with me. One year, we roomed together. I was consumed with studies to the point I would ask to have the dorm room to myself for long periods of time, and she would oblige without complaint.

"Of course," Dr. Roth continued, "she could be stubborn too. Oh! She simply would not listen to her parents when they wanted her to go into accounting or politics. She had a passion for the arts: literature, painting, music. All of it. And it was literature classes that led her to the Word."

"You did too, I'm guessing," Simon answered. If Dr. Roth had been studying languages so she could be a translator, that must have had some impact.

"Yes, I suppose so," Dr. Roth admitted. She reflected quietly for a moment, a small smile on her face.

"Thank you," Simon said sincerely. It humbled him to think of how his own life would have been different if his mom would have abandoned the λόγος and chosen the life her parents wanted. He might not have existed at all.

"She would have loved that you brought the Book of Psalms to us. She was a poet most of all, I think. In fact . . ." Dr. Roth jumped from her chair and walked to the walls of books; she trailed her hand over the lower left-hand corner of the wall to Simon's right. "Aha! Here."

She walked over and placed a small book in his hand. It was a journal, easily older than he was, and worn.

"This is a prayer journal. Abby gave it to me as a gift one year. But look on the first page."

Simon's heart beat faster as he saw handwriting he wished he knew well.

Lizzy,

Merry Christmas! Hope you use this well, and I pray that it's a blessing to you. But first, I get to use the front page. Haha!

Love, Abby

Underneath the note, Simon read the following poem.

Why do you fear the devil's reign?
    His meager power is fleeting.
Jesus has conquered death and pain,
    All Satan's minions defeating.
Now you have seen what others heard.
Here you discovered God's own Word,
    Lies and delusions unseating.

Why do you shudder in the night?
    God sends His angels' protection.
Shadows concealed are bathed in light,
    As He restores to perfection.
Wickedness seeks a place to hide;
Holiness runs to Jesus' side,
    Clinging to His resurrection.

Why do you wait with timid feet?
    Jesus' procession is leading.
The path revealed, it is complete;
    The vanquished army receding.
Fear not the one who flees the Day.
Trust in the One who is the Way,
    Guiding to mercies exceeding.

Simon didn't realize that a tear had fallen to his jawline until he finished reading it.

"It reminds me of that one passage we found."

"Yes, Matthew chapter ten. Abby used it for the text, see?"

Dr. Roth pointed to a Bible reference at the bottom of the page.

"And then it had been lost until we found it again." Simon smiled at this connection to the Word and his mom. The first time he'd heard the passage, he was standing in an alley, listening to the kindly Archivist read it to him and Jack from the vial she'd just opened. What else had she said? It was about his mom. "She was a wonderful lady. I miss her." That was it. *I do too.*

"I'll copy it down for you, Simon," Dr. Roth offered.

"That would be great. Thank you. Thanks very much, Dr. Roth." Simon was glad he finally came and asked about his mom. He'd had no idea what revelations it would bring.

"My pleasure. Then you can read it, or sing it, whenever you want."

"Sing it?"

"Sure," Dr. Roth said. She took the journal from him and began singing it to a tune he knew well. It was the tune the Messengers used when singing one of his favorite hymns. They'd sung it on the day he'd survived the Arena seven months ago. The day he witnessed to his faith in front of an entire city. The day he witnessed to his faith in the City to an entire kingdom. "Built on the Rock the Church shall stand, Even when steeples are falling." So much was falling in New Morgan. But Simon knew the Rock would not fail. And now, he had words from his mom to remind him of this truth as well.

"Of course," Dr. Roth shrugged, "you could always think of a new tune for it." She sat down and pulled a piece of paper from a work table. After a few minutes, she handed the poem to Simon.

"Now, I don't know about you, but I'm ready for some sleep," Dr. Roth said, turning off a few lanterns.

"Good night, Dr. Roth. And again, thank you."

Simon didn't sleep much that night. Instead, he read and reread his mother's words until he'd committed them to memory, finding comfort in the truth they provided. As he finally fell asleep, he had one question on his mind. *Who else can I ask about my parents?*

Chapter Seventeen

"Siiiiiiiimon. Simooooooooooon."

Simon woke long enough to groan and roll over. "Go away."

"Did you miiiiiiiiiiiss me, Simoooooooon?"

Simon heaved a sigh. "I did until just now. And if you throw water on me, so help me . . ."

"Ta-da!!!" The door swung open and slammed against the wall, but Simon only knew this by the loud crack of the metal knob on brick. He was completely buried in his covers, trying to stay warm. The December chill seeped down into Grand Station, sending its residents to pile on any quilts at their disposal.

"I see how it is," Jack moaned, allowing a chair to skid across the floor as he dragged it closer to the bed. "I spend my days and nights with the lowest of the low in New Morgan, wondering which day I'm going to have to kill or be killed, while you sleep all warm and snuggly in your blankets and can't even bring yourself to say hello!"

"Come back in an hour. I'll welcome you with bells and whistles. Go find Ella first."

"What makes you think I haven't?"

"If you had, you wouldn't be here."

Jack's laughter filled the room, and Simon admitted to himself how great it was to hear the sound.

"Touché, my friend. I shall return."

And with that, Simon's room was quiet again. After a hearty slam of the door.

"So, how long do you get to stay?" Charity asked with her gaze focused on the wall, making sure her final touches of paint would finish the eleventh disciple well.

"Just over two weeks. I have to report back the day after Christmas. Not that the military realizes that. At least, I hope they don't. When I scheduled my leave, I hoped no one was paying too much attention to those who took off this time of year."

"You all keep talking about Christmas," Simon said. "What am I supposed to know about it?"

"Right?" Ella replied. "My parents are super excited about it all, but we never celebrated it before."

Simon nodded. "I knew about the Messengers before Christmastime last year, but I was still just learning. And we weren't able to come and go as easily at the time."

Jack let out a long, low whistle. "You two don't know what you're missing."

"So, tell us about it!" Ella demanded.

"Ella," Jack said, throwing his arm around her dramatically, "I will see to it that you get to celebrate your best Christmas ever."

Ella rolled her eyes, but seemed pretty happy to stay where she was.

"So, Charity," Jack asked, looking up to the newest figure on the wall, "who is this one?"

"James. He's the brother of John."

"John? The old guy over there?"

"James died a lot earlier than John did. James was the first disciple to die, in fact. John was the last."

"That must have been hard," Ella said.

"Didn't they fight all the time, though?" Simon asked.

Charity nodded. "Yeah. Seems strange. We have some of John's Gospel. His words are really poetic. Kinda hard to imagine that Jesus called them the Sons of Thunder."

Simon mulled this over. He had some questions for Zeke. But first, Mrs. Meyer.

"Ooooh, Simon. Look at you. Skin and bones. Why on earth do you stay away from my baking so often? You aren't allergic to anything, are you? Why—"

"Hi, Mrs. Meyer. No, it's nothing like that. I'm sorry I haven't been visiting like I should."

"Here. Eat this cookie."

Simon gladly accepted the treat and took a bite. It was soft and airy, with a small bit of crunch on the edges. The cinnamon and sugar took Simon to a place that felt warm and safe. He would never understand quite how Mrs. Meyer was able to show love in such a simple way.

"There, that's better. Now, what can I do for you?"

"I have some questions I'd like to ask," Simon said, trying to enunciate around a second bite of cookie. "About my mom. And dad. And Christmas."

"My! I could talk for hours on each topic." Mrs. Meyer erupted into a hearty laugh. "Let's see. What do you say about coming up to my home for dinner tonight? I will tell you as much as we can squeeze into an evening."

"That sounds great, Mrs. Meyer," Simon said. "Thank you."

"Come back here around seven this evening, and we'll head up together. Now. Take a few more cookies to go. Share them with your friends."

Simon walked through the tunnels of the City and considered what the evening would hold. He had been in Mrs. Meyer's home only once, and he was saddened at the memory. The dimly lit room, the harrowing sounds of death. The fact that of the four who were in that room, only two were still alive. Simon looked forward to spending time with the cheery Mrs. Meyer, but he was afraid of what might lurk in the shadows for him that evening.

He wasn't the only one, he knew, who faced dark memories, and he was on a search to help another. Through the dark tunnels, he carefully wound his way with the aid of his flashlight. He had only a hunch that he would be successful, but he hoped he was right. Otherwise, he'd have journeyed to a remote and dark place for little reason.

Simon held his breath when he saw the first skull. He knew it would be the perfect time to exact revenge on the person he sought, but this was neither the time nor the place. Out of respect for those who would one day rise up with him, he didn't dare pull anything irreverent. Besides, if he was right . . .

He was. As Simon found the back corner of the catacombs, he saw Jack sitting on the floor, facing the coffin.

"I'm sorry you lost him, Simon."

Simon was startled that Jack knew he was there. But after all, if Simon knew where Jack would be, maybe Jack knew Simon just as well.

"I am too." Simon came near the head of his dad's coffin and sat down.

"He was a great Postmaster. And pastor. I guess I kinda thought of him as my own pastor," Jack admitted. "I miss him."

Simon didn't realize how much his dad had meant to Jack until the first time he saw the Bible passage.

"Is that why you visit the coffin?"

Jack shrugged. "I know he's not here. But coming here helps me focus."

Simon couldn't help but chuckle. "I don't think that's the reaction most people would have walking among thousands of bones."

"That's just it. I mean, sure, I come because of your dad. I want to be sure no one's messed with his grave like others did for all these people. They're gonna need these bones again someday. I wish we could have done a better job of protecting them."

Simon nodded. "But ultimately, that's God's job. And His promise. If Job's bones will rise again, God's got everyone else covered too."

"Job?"

"I saw it once in the marketplace's album. Job lived long before Jesus, so he's definitely dust now. But in his lifetime, he saw really amazing times and unbelievably terrible times. At one of his lowest moments, though, he says, 'After my skin has been thus destroyed, yet in my flesh I shall see God, whom I shall see for myself, and my eyes shall behold, and not another.' It's in Job chapter nineteen."

Jack looked up at the skeletal remains that surrounded them. "Simon, how many skeletons am I going to have to make? I know governments war and all that. But we both know Revemond hasn't done anything wrong. I'd rather lose my own life for this stunt New Morgan is pulling than take others."

Simon didn't know what to say.

"Have you begun to fight yet?"

Jack shook his head. "No. We've only been training so far. And getting brainwashed, of course. Not like most of us needed any more brainwashing. We're graduates of Preparatory School, after all," he scoffed. "Your uncle would be great at it, though. Hey, where is he, anyway?"

Simon frowned. "I have no idea. And I hope to keep it that way."

"Simon?" Jack asked. "What's going to happen? This war is going to happen. And we know that New Morgan's claim to be a world power is ludicrous. But what if we lose?"

Simon shuddered at a different question. "What if we win?"

Mrs. Meyer was mysteriously quiet as she saw Simon enter the Room of the Martyrs. Her table was already cleared for the evening. She greeted him with a grin and a beckoning wave as she turned toward the corner door that led to tunnels and, ultimately, her home. She had one small bag in her hand, which she refused to let him carry.

"Now," she said, as she opened the door, "you'll have to help me cook tonight since I didn't have anything planned." Her chuckle made it clear that Simon's impromptu request was more than welcome.

"Here we are." Mrs. Meyer guided Simon into the house and threw the dead bolt on the door behind her. She closed another door, which looked like a closet, to conceal the way to the City. "Come to the kitchen now, and I'll put you to work."

In no time, Simon was dicing red potatoes that were given, he was told, by Mr. Saunders in the main marketplace. "He simply would not let me pay more than a fraction of what they were worth." She had opened a can of chicken chunks and was applying spices to the pieces now that they were drained and rinsed. "This mix was given to me by Macee. Do you know Macee?" Next, Simon grated a large carrot that Mrs. Meyer evidently grew out of her kitchen window box. "Can you believe it? I thought for sure there would be no sun at all in that little spot, but here it is!" In no time, Mrs. Meyer was stirring a soup with an incredible aroma that wafted throughout the kitchen.

"Mrs. Meyer, I don't think I've smelled anything this delicious in my entire life."

"Oh, Simon! I hope that isn't true," she said, wiping her hands on a towel that hung on the cabinet handle. "This is just a simple dish I used to have when I was a child. Of course, back then, we also had garlic and chives—now, listen to me. This'll do, won't it?"

After one bite, Simon was certain that this was the best meal he had ever eaten, and he marveled how Mrs. Meyer was able to take the same government-issued goods he had once received and create something that brought, well, joy.

"So, Simon, I know you didn't come here for a bowl of soup," she said with a laugh. "Let's see what kind of answers I can give you. Your parents . . . where do I even begin? I went to college at about the same time they did, and we always seemed to bump into each other from time to time over the years. Jonathan, my, he was a catch! Not unlike you," she said with a quick wink, "but of course you look like your mother. Anyway, there were quite a few ladies who pined for your father, but he only had eyes for Abigail. No wonder. She was a delight. It's no surprise to you that they fell madly in love with each other. Her parents had a fit, to be sure. Poor little Juliet. Oh, that's right. You haven't read that one, have you? No matter. Your parents were a match made in heaven."

Mrs. Meyer took a bite of her cooling soup wistfully before diving back into her story.

"After college, we all still kept in touch over the Internet—you know, before it was taken over by New Morgan. Your father was brilliant, simply brilliant, mind you. I'd be willing to bet he'd be a professor at the seminary right now if it wasn't a pile of rubble. And, well . . ." She took a sip of water and hurried on.

"My point, of course, is that you have every reason to be proud of your parents and thankful for two such fine people to be chosen by God to raise you. If you haven't noticed," Mrs. Meyer said while giving his arm a light tap, "I've taken quite a liking to you. And not just because I think so much of Jon and Abby. No, Simon, God's been pruning you. And He's been giving you everything you need. That's true for us all, of course, but—oh, how do I put this? I can't wait to see the man you'll become someday."

Simon swallowed his last spoonful of soup and felt the heat rise to his face. He knew better than to think his parents—or he—were flawless. But it was encouraging nevertheless to hear kind words about people he loved and missed terribly.

"I'm not sure which is worse," Simon admitted. "Feeling the pain of missing my dad, who was the person I knew best, or feeling hollow about my mom and missing the person I never knew."

Mrs. Meyer smiled against the tears that formed in her eyes, and her silence spoke volumes.

"Are you doing okay, Mrs. Meyer? After Mr. Meyer passed away?"

Mrs. Meyer took a large drink of water before answering. "Oh, I imagine you understand better than most, Simon. I'll always miss him. Nothing will change that. It hurts when people talk about him. It hurts when people don't talk about him. Either way, I have to remember that people mean well. And I certainly know I'm loved. So many people reached out and cared for me right after his death. And they still love me, of course. Even though time marches on. I'm comforted knowing that George is with the Lord. And the Lord is with me. Nothing can change either of those two things, and I have true hope in the future. What more can I ask?"

Both let the silence fall on the room as Mrs. Meyer finished her soup, now long cold.

"Let's see," she finally said. "What else did you ask? Ah yes! Christmas! Oh, it's a lovely time. Now, it's much simpler in the City than it was when I was your age. But you know? In some ways, I like that more. But before I begin," she said, jumping up and reaching for the bag she had brought home that evening, "let's get started on this."

And with that, she pulled out the most beautiful dessert Simon had ever seen.

With one of her brightest smiles, Mrs. Meyer declared, "It's time for pie."

Chapter Eighteen

He stared at the door. It had been months since he had arranged for such a meeting, and his faculty had noticed. He knew he had no choice but to return to status quo, or else suspicion would rise among those in authority. He could lose his job. Or worse.

But why did he hesitate? This is what he lived for: changing the world, one life at a time. He was gradually, patiently showing wayward young minds how treacherously their parents had misled them all their lives. After painstaking care, it took him only a year to bring them to the light out of the darkness of regressive, superstitious thinking.

Most of the time.

He cringed when he thought of who might be on the other side of the door. If it was a normal youth, he would have no trouble at all conforming the simple mind to one more suited for society.

And yet.

If the student were devious, monstrous, almost genius in his rhetoric, so that long after you thought your job was complete, he comes and challenges you and smiles in the face of death for—for what? What was it that made him so confident? so arrogant? Just like his parents. What could possibly motivate them to run counter to society even if doing so could remove them from the world entirely?

Enough. If anyone came down, they would see him standing in front of the door, doing nothing at all.

Roderick Druck turned the knob and opened the door. A small stone room with a tall ceiling greeted him. A glance up at the small window confirmed that it was still raining. Good. Less of a chance for eavesdroppers. A petite female with red hair and wide eyes stared at him from the wooden table, and he conjured his widest smile.

To his horror, she smiled back.

"Merry Christmas." Charity and Simon were sitting in the middle of a tunnel, under the glow of two lanterns. Charity had just handed him a small package wrapped in paper, neatly tied with a thin string.

The package felt heavy and was in the shape of a square about the length of his hand. He pulled the string away and unfolded the paper. He took out a square piece of clay and turned it over. On the other side, glass pieces glowed in the lantern light.

"A mosaic!"

"My very first."

In the center of the square, a cross was surrounded by an orange glow. The cross was a bold dark brown, and wrapped around it were vivid green vines and bright red and golden fruit. The border of the mosaic was gold, reminiscent of gates, laden with jewels. Simon recognized the patterns immediately.

"Like the mosaics on either side of the Elders' room."

Charity smiled and nodded. "Only here, Lucifer is nowhere to be found."

Simon smiled. "I can't wait for that to be a reality. Charity, it's beautiful. How did you get it done?"

"I've been visiting the hallways and studying. It's just my first try, and it could be better—"

"I love it. Thank you," Simon assured her. "The only problem is, I didn't wrap your gift. I guess I missed that part." Mrs. Meyer had gone into great detail about the traditions of celebrating Christmas when she was a child, but he must have become distracted when the details of gift delivery came into the discussion. "Okay, so, hold out your hands. And close your eyes."

Charity complied, and Simon took a moment to study her. Her beauty was breathtaking. He had been captured by her since the time they met, and now that he knew so much of what lay underneath, his respect and amazement of her only grew.

"Uh, Simon?"

"Right. Here it is." Simon quickly pulled something out of his back pocket and gently placed it in her waiting hands. "Okay, ready."

Charity opened her eyes and immediately smiled. She held up the small gift and examined it. A flat wooden disc was in the middle with two thin leather straps fastened on either side. She brought the bracelet closer to her face and studied the design.

"Dad was always good at carving," Simon explained, a lump in his throat. "I thought I'd use some of his tools I still had and give it a try." He knew she would instantly recognize the symbol. It was the Chi-Rho, but with a very faint star behind it. It was the symbol Charity had taken to declare her freedom. On the other side, he had written a Bible reference.

"John chapter eight, verse thirty-six," she read.

"'So if the Son sets you free, you will be free indeed,'" Simon recited. "Something new to wear on your arm."

Charity threw her arms around Simon, and he was shocked to hear her openly cry. Another first for Charity. He held her tight until she let go.

"It's perfect. Thank you."

"Merry Christmas," he answered.

The service had an air of mystery and beauty about it as the readings talked about the coming Lord and their anticipation of the Last Day. The Messengers had been preparing for this day for weeks, and Simon could feel the momentum build as everyone gathered together to sing of a God who would descend to the earth to become man out of love for His people. They sang of messengers of the truth, of the Word become flesh, of the Light of the world.

Simon and Charity sat by Mrs. Meyer, who continued to teach quietly. "We always sang this one when I was a little girl. Oh, this one I didn't learn until after Chin introduced it a few years ago. He reminds me of my pastor when I was young. Did you know, he used to write a new hymn stanza every Christmas, and . . ."

Simon enjoyed every minute, and as midnight came, the singing grew louder in celebration of God's promise revealed in a child, the Son of David, the Son of God.

When the service ended, Simon didn't know what else could make the night better.

"Merry Christmas!" Ella spouted as she bounced toward their pew. Without hesitation, she grabbed Simon's hand and dropped a note into it. Then she was off to join her parents and Jack.

Simon unrolled the piece of paper and marveled at the gift as he held it open for him and Charity to read. Ella's handwriting presented a copied message.

Dear Simon,

It pains us to hear news of Jonathan, but we do not mourn without hope. We speak every night to the One on the throne about you, and we think of you often. Whether the trumpets sound or whether Jericho falls, we will see you again.

With Charity,
Caleb and Jane

"With Charity?" Simon puzzled. "I didn't mention you. I didn't think it was safe."

"*Charity* is another word for love," she answered.

"I should have known."

"Simon?"

It was three nights after Christmas, and Simon had just gotten into bed, so a knock on the door and someone calling his name came as a surprise.

"Come in."

Chin opened the door, fully dressed in dark clothing. Simon sat up, curious.

"Is there a Carrier job?" he asked.

"No, a pastor's job. I was hoping you would come with me to the Pharens' home."

Simon suddenly felt cold. There were several reasons why Simon thought he should be the last person to visit the Pharens. Yet, he felt the responsibility of friendship tugging at him. Besides, he wasn't one to turn down a mission.

"I'll be ready in five minutes."

Chin led them to the Room of the Martyrs, making their way toward the South Gate. "There has been a great deal of military activity near City Hall," he explained. Simon wondered if Jack was in those ranks.

He passed the mural that included his mom's image and gave it a small nod on his way to the tunnel. The tunnel torches illumined the symbols he saw on his first visit to the City a little more than a year ago. As he passed the Chi-Rho, he thought of Charity, glad she was safely sleeping in the heart of the City.

Judah stood guard at the South Gate tonight, and he unbolted the locks for them. "God be with you," he whispered as he opened the door.

"Amen," Chin replied.

The night breeze felt refreshing—it had been a while since Simon had been on a mission. Midnight walks had been unnecessary since they had finished delivering the Book of Psalms to the Archives of Westbend. He wasn't sure if he was imagining it, but his leg felt stronger too. He just hoped he wouldn't have to test it too much tonight.

Chin and Simon weaved in and out of the streets. They'd heard the low growl of a Bot motor several blocks away, but it hadn't come near. They saw a light from a Security flashlight once, but it had not found them crouching behind stacked crates.

The real trepidation Simon felt was reaching their destination. At last, they arrived at 2351 Merchant Street. As Chin opened the front building door, Simon looked behind them to glance at 2350. Its darkened windows stared back, hollow and lifeless.

The two entered the building and took the stairs up to the Pharen apartment. After one soft knock, the door opened. Mrs. Pharen scowled at her visitors, but she moved to the side to let them in. After closing and locking the door behind them, she escaped to her bedroom without uttering a word.

Dr. Pharen was lying on one of the couches in their living room area, covered in blankets. He smiled weakly as Chin and Simon approached.

"Dr. Pharen, it is good to see you," Chin said, kneeling on the floor near him.

"Please. Call me Arnold."

Dr. Pharen then coughed and winced in pain after, a haunting reminder for Simon of Mr. Meyer. This could not be happening. *Not Dr. Pharen.* Simon felt burdened with guilt at all he'd put the Pharens through. They had been the family to watch him when his mother was captured. And he'd been a burden to them ever since.

"Arnold, how are you feeling?" Chin asked.

Dr. Pharen gave a melancholy smile. "Not well, I'm afraid. I've known it for some time, but my body simply is not what it used to be. There are treatments, I know, in other countries. But here . . ." he trailed off.

Simon had been standing at a distance, but he was overcome with emotion and knelt beside Chin, looking Dr. Pharen in the eye.

"Dr. Pharen, this is all my fault. I've caused you stress and grief that you didn't deserve. It's my fault you're doing so poorly. I'm so, so sorry."

Dr. Pharen gave a weak laugh, grimacing again at the effort.

"Nonsense, Simon. On the contrary, you've given me much hope. It has been a blessing for me to see your changes over the past year, even if from afar. I'd been concerned for you, but I now see how hypocritical I was. No, Simon. Nothing you did made me unwell. I've been sick for some time. Even so, Simon. Truly, I wish I could have helped your father."

"I know. There was nothing you could have done. Please, don't let it worry you anymore."

"Elder Chin," Dr. Pharen said, "I have much to confess. Oh, I have so many regrets. My family has been lukewarm these past two decades, and the Messengers suffered for it. Look at our home." He gestured to the comparatively lavish furnishings that filled their apartment. "Extra medical attention to high-ranking officials. Sitting on the fence. We claimed to believe in the Word, yet we risked nothing for it. We allowed fear to justify our behavior. And I let it all happen. I . . . modeled it, even." Dr. Pharen paused while he looked bleakly at the ceiling.

"Simon," he said, turning toward him, "you helped me. You reminded me that the Message is worth dying for. You reminded me that loss is worth the eternal prize. I'm so sorry for not being a better neighbor to you and Jonathan. There was so much we could have done."

Simon shook his head. He wanted to quiet Dr. Pharen and tell him that everything was okay, but he could see the urgency in Dr. Pharen's face. He could tell how important it was for him to say these things.

"And Elder Chin, that is not all . . ."

Movement out of the corner of Simon's eye distracted him, and he saw Ben appear at the doorway into the main living space. Ben's face was blank, unmoving.

Simon stood up and walked toward Ben, who retreated a few steps back into the hallway. Simon instinctively paused, but not for long. It was time to be a good neighbor.

He followed Ben to his room. Ben sat on his bed, and Simon sat on a chair near the door.

"You got us into trouble again."

"Ella told me. That must have been hard to keep quiet."

"Oh, I'm good at keeping quiet," Ben snapped. "You're the one who has a problem."

"I'm sorry, Ben. You were so excited when those other messages came out—"

"We didn't get in trouble for those."

"That's because they weren't real."

Ben growled in frustration. "Simon! Do you have to have an answer for everything?!"

Simon was silent. This annoyed Ben too, who continued.

"You think you're so smart. You're like the hero of the Messengers or something. Well, let me tell you something. You ditched us. You completely forgot about the Word for, like, almost two years. And now you're the big shot who gets all the attention. And the rest of us get in trouble!"

"Ben, I can't tell you how sorry I am that I forgot the Message. It will haunt me for the rest of my life." Simon spoke slowly. He didn't trust his own emotions, much less Ben's. "And I'm trying to learn what the right thing to do is when it comes to the Messengers and New Morgan. But I gotta tell ya. It seems like no matter what I do, it's a mistake. It's a lose-lose situation, and I'm tired of trying to figure out what will help others without angering New Morgan. I'm pretty sure there's no way around it."

There was a moment of silence, which Simon hoped was progress.

"I'm praying for your dad."

That was a mistake. Ben practically spat his response.

"What's the use?! God didn't save your mom. Or your dad. Why would He save mine?"

The words wounded Simon, and he responded with the earnestness of someone who feared for his friend.

"Ben, He did save them. All of them. Thousands of years ago. Yes, death is rough. I think it's safe to say I know that full well. But when our lives are eternal, the time or place of our death doesn't matter so much as the time and place of our life after that—and the time is forever. The place is worth everything we might go through here."

Simon couldn't believe the words that were coming out of his mouth, but he knew they were true. The timing of someone's death matters to those who are left on earth. But eventually, the earthy timeline will be a speck in comparison to eternity. The surprise isn't that death happens. The surprise is that life happens. And continues to happen.

Ben folded his arms, scanning his room. His eyes rested on something that prompted him to stand up.

"Here. I was at the library a while back, and the librarian wanted you to have this." An edge of disdain and jealousy laced the sentence.

Simon took the book that Ben had taken from his dresser and shoved Simon's way. The title was faded, but the large letters could still be seen: *The History of the Early Church*. Simon thumbed through it. It reminded Simon that Ben had offered several months ago to help with research. Simon realized that Ben was fulfilling that promise in spite of himself.

"Did you read any of it?" Simon asked. He hoped he had.

Ben shrugged. "A few pages. Seems like believers were always on the run," he said with disgust. "Is there never a time they won something?!"

"Ben, Jesus has already won everything. What more could you want?"

Chapter Nineteen

Simon's step was heavy as he walked back to the City with Chin. He had spoken more with Dr. Pharen and parted ways with bittersweet joy.

"I'm afraid I can't visit the City right now, and Ben chooses not to go alone," he lamented. Chin assured him that the Elders would take turns visiting when they could.

Simon's parting with Ben didn't end as well, with strained silence eventually leading Simon out of Ben's room. It was his turn to worry about his neighbor. The sky was bright, which of course meant that the moonlight could reveal their movements to Security. Chin and Simon were halfway to the City when they stopped dead in their tracks.

Silently, a Bot passed at the end of the alley just ahead of them. It was sleek, and its engine purred with quiet menace. Chin and Simon froze, and Simon hoped against all reason that they had not been seen. A light flashed on, blinding them both, and Chin spun around.

"RUN!"

Simon raced behind Chin and turned in the opposite direction of the Elder as they came to the end of the alley. Pain began to throb in his leg, but he did his best to ignore it, pushing himself as fast as he could go.

After a few blocks, Simon looked up and found his bearings until *wham!*

He'd run smack into the back of a Security guard who had been hiding in the shadows of a street corner. The Security guard looked surprisingly young to Simon, and he seemed just as surprised as Simon to have made a capture. He grabbed Simon's arm and began blowing a whistle. Simon wrenched his arm free, barreling through to the next alley, knowing that others would be in pursuit behind him in no time. Simon didn't know what direction he was going anymore, and he fought pain and exhaustion as he heard whistles, shouts, and even the growl of motors grow behind him. *I'm doomed. It's over.* Simon was about to give up when he saw a tall man with ebony skin appear in front of him. *Malachi!*

Simon ran straight to him and would have given him a huge hug if not for the forces of New Morgan chasing from behind.

"Follow me."

Simon obeyed, taking every dodge and turn that Malachi made. Halfway down one alley, Malachi pulled open a door and walked right in. A knot of panic gripped Simon, but he knew better than to think twice. He ducked inside the entrance as Malachi closed the door. They were in a tiny room with absolutely no furnishings or decorations. Parallel to the door they just entered was another door, but Malachi didn't open it. They simply waited in silence. Malachi was stoic, as if standing guard before a royal throne room. While Simon was initially restless in the quiet waiting, Malachi exuded confidence and peace. It was contagious, and Simon felt his heart gradually slow down.

After a lapse of time that Simon couldn't discern, Malachi opened the door and stepped back out into the night. The rest of the journey home was calm and uneventful. As they neared the North Gate, Simon remembered Chin's warning, but he wasn't afraid.

"Thank you, Malachi, for always being there. Even when I don't deserve it."

A curious smile passed over Malachi's face, but he nodded. Malachi stopped at the corner near the North Gate to stand guard, and Simon slipped back into the City, greeted by Michael at the door.

Ella stared at the paper. She sat on the counter of the cellar, which was only lit near the entranceway. They rarely came into this room now that Spence had been captured, but it was a good place to be alone. Charity and Simon stood on either side of her, reading the note in Ella's hand.

```
Dear Ella,
I don't know how I'll get this to
you, but I'll find a way. We've
been fighting for two weeks, and
```

```
it's been bad. Clearly, the rest
of the world has kept advancing
while we're stuck in the past.
Captain Sprangler noticed I had a
way with words, so he appointed me
as his secretary. I'm safe, but I
don't think New Morgan is. If they
found this letter, I'd probably be
charged with treason. Ah, well. It
could be worse! I miss you.
Yours,
Jack
```

"It's so . . . sweet," Charity said, almost in bewilderment.

"And not sarcastic. Well, not very," Simon agreed.

"Something's wrong," Ella concluded.

"Well sure, Ella. He's in a war," Simon said, giving poor comfort.

"We've gotta do something," Ella insisted.

"Like what? Kidnap a soldier? Stop a war?" Simon protested.

"I don't know, Simon, okay?! Just something. Anything! When I met you, you were out saving the world every other day, finding the Message and sending it far and wide. Don't you miss that?! I spent hours on end to create this thing," she said, motioning wildly at the silent Bot behind her. "And it's just sitting there! Don't you want to do something again? Don't you want to make a difference?"

"Ella, what are you suggesting?" Charity asked.

"I don't know. I don't. But this machine is quiet, fast, and ready to *do something*, for crying out loud! Isn't there a place we could go to get more passages from the Word? Could we try Centra?"

Simon thought about it. "It would be great if this could take to the streets at night without being caught, but Centra is too far away. And they didn't have the Word like we do." Simon suddenly pitied them for their lack of any spiritual support. No pastors. No Scripture. Why was it that Westbend had more resources? Chin gave a few reasons, but the massacre stood out foremost in his mind.

"Okay, Ella," Charity soothed. "We'll think of something, okay? Let's just all think about it and see if we can come up with a plan. Once we figure something out, we'll meet back here."

Ella nodded, but didn't say anything. She took the note, folded it carefully, and placed it in a pocket. Worry lined her face.

"'Why are you cast down, O my soul, and why are you in turmoil within me?'" Simon quoted; he had no more words of his own. "'Hope in God; for I shall again praise Him, my salvation and my God.' Psalm forty-two."

Ella took a deep breath and nodded. She hopped down from the counter and started walking out of the cellar.

"Until next time," she said with determination.

"Zeke?" Simon had never been to his room in the City, and he hoped he hadn't knocked on the wrong door. Almost immediately, however, the door swung open, and Zeke looked up at Simon with curiosity. "Simon, my boy! Come in, come in."

Simon entered and marveled at the sparse room. A small bed with a simple blanket stood against the far wall, one of the only items in the room. Simon sat on the floor and leaned his back on the wall near the door. Without hesitation, Zeke sat cross-legged across from him.

"So, I've been thinking about James and John," Simon began.

"Ah yes. The Sons of Thunder! My, those two must have been a handful. Always quarreling, vying to be the very best. Their own mother once asked Jesus to set them next to Him on His throne! Haha! If only she knew what she was asking! But, on the other hand, those two were very close to Jesus. Peter, James, and John were the three Jesus always called on for special occasions. Well, that's not to say they were perfect. Goodness, look at Peter. But even so. John stayed by Jesus at the cross, and Jesus gave His own mother, Mary, into John's care."

"But when you read John's writings," Simon said, "he seems . . . calmer."

"Ah, well, you may have a point there," Zeke said, his eyes squinting in concentration. "But there are some things you must know about John. First, James, his brother, was the very first disciple to die. Herod killed him by the sword. Second, John was the last of the disciples to die. It seems he was the only one who had not been martyred. John lived many, many years. And he outlived many, many believers. He saw brothers and sisters in Christ die year after year, and that must have taken its toll. And late in his life, he was banished to live on the island of Patmos. Which brings me to my third point. John's writings came when he was an old man. He saw himself as a father to the next generation, and so that surely shaped the way he wrote."

Simon considered this. "So that makes sense . . . why the Gospel of John sounds different from the other Gospels."

Zeke nodded. "The other three Gospels came out early, so everyone could know the truth of the promised Savior, the Son of David. John's Gospel tells the same account, but there's a sense of poetry, of explanation to it all."

Simon recalled one of his favorites from the first chapter of John's Gospel. "'The light shines in the darkness, and the darkness has not overcome it.' You know, John would have fit in well in New Morgan!" Simon said, smiling.

"No doubt about that," Zeke said. "It was difficult for the believers of that time. In many times, to be sure."

"That was another question I had," Simon said eagerly. "I've been reading this book on the history of the Early Church. Have things always been tough for believers?"

"Hmmm," Zeke said. "I suppose that depends on who you ask. For example, remember what happened with Stephen?"

"Sure, he was stoned to death."

"And what happened next?"

Simon tried to remember.

"Did the believers stop spreading the Message?" Zeke pressed.

"No."

"No! Exactly! Now, I'm sure there were plenty who became scared and turned away. But others wondered about a Message that could be worth dying for."

"So the Church has always had hard times."

"Again, it depends on the way you look at it. There are other times when life looked pretty cushy for believers. But during those times, the church sometimes attracted those who were more interested in the power and riches than the priceless treasure. Even believers would get distracted and forget the importance of service, love, and the Bible."

"Kind of like in Morganland."

"In a way, yes. Like I've told you before: Satan is the worst kind of trickster. In places where it is easy to believe, it is also easy to take faith for granted. Where it's difficult, well, that's when believers take things more seriously. So to answer your question: when things seem hard for believers, that's often when they're the most Christlike. After all, Jesus came to serve and to suffer for all. When things seem easy, that's when Satan lays other traps, such as laziness and unbelief and—"

"Fighting?" Simon had Ben in mind, but he quickly realized that he could create a list of conflicts he'd witnessed among the Messengers, many of which he'd been a part of.

"Well, now, I think we're coming back to John again," Zeke said, a glimmer in his eye. He hopped up and grabbed a stack of papers from his nightstand. "John wrote his Gospel, but he also wrote three letters. We have one of them . . ."

"Sure. We read from First John all the time."

"Quite right. And there was another book too. The Book of Revelation. We don't have that one, I'm afraid. Anyway, John's books and letters were filled with love. Literally. He used the word *love* more than the other Gospels combined, and it was all over his epistles! Here, for example—chapter four of his first letter: 'Beloved, let us love one another, for love is from God, and whoever loves has been born of God and knows God. Anyone who does not love does not know God, because God is love.' Oh! Now, this is a good one—same letter, but in chapter two: 'Whoever hates his brother is in the darkness and walks in the darkness, and does not know where he is going, because the darkness has blinded his eyes.'"

Zeke had been reading from his stack of handwritten papers, his own copy of the passages the Messengers had found. Simon's mental list of conflicts definitely had some highlights now: Micah, Spence, and also Ben.

"I can't help but wonder," Zeke said, stroking his chin, "if John thought of James when he was writing. If, after all his years of watching others die, he wanted everyone else to understand that quarrels only lead to harm. That love is the fulfillment of the Law."

As usual, time had flown while talking with Zeke. But Simon's yawns reminded him of the hour.

"Thanks, Zeke. You've given me a lot more to think about."

Zeke laughed heartily. "Splendid! That's what I'm here for."

Chapter Twenty

One by one. One by one, my brothers have lost their lives for the Way.

And I am still here. Peter had asked, hadn't he? He had asked Jesus what would happen to me. Jesus refused to tell us. But here I am, the last of the disciples. The disciple whom Jesus loved.

Love. I have seen so much death, and I have seen so many disagreements and fighting—for what? It was the trick of Satan, of course, to keep us from spreading the Word. But the Word will not be stopped. In the beginning was the Word, and the Word was with God, and the Word was God. So I will continue to share the Word, and I will write it down so that others may believe that Jesus is the Christ, the Son of God, that they may believe and have life in His name.

■ ■ ■

Simon sat in the cellar, waiting for Ella and Charity. Ella came first and sat on the floor, leaning against the front of the counter. Charity joined right after and took a seat on the stairs near Simon.

"Okay," Ella said. "What've we got?"

"Well," Charity started, "the question about writing messages is whether or not it's effective. But people are paying attention, right? They have to be. That's how the Word works—it's powerful that way. So what if we create a message no one can ignore? We spread the word to all the Messengers—every single one. On the same night, every believer comes out of the shadows and shares the Word. There's no way New Morgan can erase them all."

Ella nodded slowly. "Then what?"

Charity shrugged. "I dunno. We keep doing it? We think of other ideas? It's about time the truth was revealed to the entire city."

"Okay, I like that," Ella answered. "So, what do you think, Simon?"

"Yeah, we need to reveal the truth about the λόγος. And we also need to reveal the truth about New Morgan. On our way back from Centra, we stayed in an abandoned warehouse filled with all of the pamphlets New Morgan used to desensitize everyone. By bringing attention to them all at the same time, maybe people will realize that they've been duped all these years. I say we grab the pamphlets and toss them all over—like confetti from the rooftops or something."

Ella mulled this one over and then asked, "How are we going to get to the top of buildings?"

Simon shrugged. "I didn't get that far yet. Maybe we figure out which Messengers live in apartments that are up a few floors. Or maybe we just do what we do best: Walk the streets, but drop them everywhere we go."

"That could work," Ella agreed. "Or we could use a little stealth," she added, gesturing to the large silhouette behind her. "At least, that's what my plan uses. This beauty hasn't even gotten its first drive. I—I was waiting for Spence before we tried it out, but . . ."

"So, what's the plan?" Charity asked, trying for a distraction.

Ella shook herself slightly, as if casting away the sadness that threatened her. "We take this Bot on a trip. It can go two, maybe three, hours without needing charging, so we should see what kinds of towns are within reach. Maybe the smaller towns don't get as much supervision. Maybe, just maybe, there are some places with the Scriptures hidden."

"What options are there?" Charity asked.

"Dad once mentioned a town called Shoreton," Simon shrugged. The only time it was mentioned was when Jonathon spoke of Abigail's last days, and Simon hoped it wasn't their only option. "Centra's definitely out, as we said. First of all, it's too far. Plus, Chin said Westbend was always more likely to have a Messenger presence anyway."

"Why?" Ella asked.

"Because . . ." Simon tried to remember. "Because . . . oh! Yes! Why didn't I think about that before?"

"Simon?" Charity interrupted. "Where are we going?"

"Friends," Simon said grandly, "we're going to the seminary."

"Isn't the seminary gone?"

"Destroyed. Nothing but rubble," Simon reported to Charity after they had walked Ella to the South Gate.

"That's kind of a drawback, don't you think?"

"You know, the more I think about it, the more I like the idea. If the seminary were still intact, it would probably be gutted with a huge black scorch mark still on the ground where the massive book bonfire had taken place. But since the building was knocked down, maybe they didn't even bother to check what was inside. Maybe there's all kinds of things concealed under a pile of bricks and mortar and wood."

"Sounds dangerous."

"Sounds worth it," Simon countered.

"You know I'm going with you, don't you?"

Simon shot her a pained look.

"The Bot has only two seats, pretty sure."

"Ah, well. Miss me while I'm gone," Charity said with a smile.

"You have no resident papers!"

"Neither do you. And you're public enemy number one, remember?"

Simon could see this conversation was getting him nowhere. "First things first. We need to organize a giant propaganda party, right?"

"Sounds like a good idea to me," Charity said, slowing down as they neared the resident quarters. "That way, we can test out the Bot in the city streets and see how it does. But we'll need help. We'll need others on foot, and maybe we can use that truck you all rode in before."

Simon nodded. The truck would be the riskiest. It was slow, noisy, and hard to hide. But it would be able to carry a huge amount of published lies.

"Hey, has Ella mentioned anything about . . . the war?" Simon asked.

Charity frowned and shook her head. They were near a set of stairs, and she took a seat. "From what I've heard in the marketplace, all the news reports say we're winning. But have you heard it? Late at night, I can't help but think that I'm hearing explosions—or feeling them. They're far off . . . for now."

Simon swallowed. He wasn't sure if it had been his imagination, but he'd noticed the same thing.

"Which means we're losing," he said, sitting beside her.

"Which means New Morgan is losing."

Simon thought of Jack. "It's still our government, you know."

"It is. And I attempt to keep the law as much as it's in my power. Of course, my mere existence is illegal . . ."

Simon smiled. He couldn't help but appreciate that Charity's biting wit rivaled his own sardonic humor.

"And New Morgan will continue to be my country. Until it isn't."

Simon laughed. "Fair enough. Let's just hope Jack's not too close to the front."

Charity's demeanor instantly changed, and she nodded solemnly.

"Simon? If Revemond takes over New Morgan, do you think things will be better?"

"You know, Charity, I have no idea," Simon admitted. "It sure seems that way, from the little I know about it. But I keep thinking about what Zeke told me recently. The devil has a trick for Messengers no matter where they are. And in this world, no place is perfect."

"A simple 'probably' would have been okay," Charity confessed grimly.

"Sorry," Simon said, stretching to get up. "I'm sure it'll be just swell."

"I'll take it. Good night, Simon."

"Till tomorrow, Charity."

The next few days passed quickly. Simon was amazed at how easy it was to gain support for their next mission. Word spread throughout the City that any willing Carriers and other Messengers who were trained for midnight missions were to gather three blocks east of the South Gate on Friday night. Simon, Chin, and Malachi would load the papers from the warehouse to the truck and meet Ella, the Bot, and others at the rendezvous point. Simon was excited for another way to reveal New Morgan's deception to the public, but this was their largest endeavor yet. The last attempt even remotely this large cost them Spence and Cyril. Simon could only hope they were still alive somewhere.

"We have searched everywhere in our power," Zeke told all volunteers in a gathering on Thursday. "And yet, we have had no success in locating either Spence or Elder Cyril. We've lost other brave Messengers this year, and I cannot stress enough the danger you will face tomorrow night. If you choose not to participate, we will understand. If you do, I beg you all to be careful."

Friday flew by, and it was nearly time for Simon to meet Chin and Malachi in the Room of the Martyrs. But first, he visited the Room of the Twelve.

"So, what'll you do when you're finished with them all?"

Charity looked up at James, who was nearly finished, and the empty space beside him. "I suppose I could find a place for Matthias and Paul," she said thoughtfully. "Or maybe I'll move on to mosaics."

She climbed down the ladder and absently dropped her paintbrush bristle-end up in her pocket. Simon took her in and was suddenly at a loss for words. Each mission became more difficult.

Charity's eyes softened, and Simon wondered how much of his mind she could read. She stepped forward and placed her hand on his right cheek. "Be safe out there tonight," she pleaded.

"You too," he replied, his voice breaking. He wrapped his arms tightly around her and kissed her for what he prayed would not be the last time. Before letting her go, he ran his hand through the black-and-red hair that had first captured his notice in the Arena a lifetime ago. He closed his eyes and said a prayer for her, and for everyone risking their lives for the truth. Without another word, he headed toward the Room of the Martyrs.

Chapter Twenty-One

The warehouse loomed silently in the night, and Simon realized that this part of the mission would be more difficult than in the daytime. They would need flashlights even in the office. With such high windows in the main space, the lights would not likely be detected as they carried their cargo to the truck, but they would have more to juggle with less visibility while working.

Chin opened a door to the right of the loading dock's big overhead doors and led the group inside to complete darkness.

"Here." A light came on, and Malachi raised it to his head. It was a work hat with a light on the front. He handed two others to his partners.

Simon turned his light on and looked around. His beam quickly found the truck parked in the loading area. He had mixed feelings about the vehicle before him, and he was glad to move on into the large, open room on the other side of the door Jack had found months ago.

"Don't look up," Malachi advised quietly. Of course, Simon instantly wanted to do just that, but he knew the reason: this was the room with the high windows. They walked across the expansive room quickly. Chin found a dolly, and Malachi found a cart, which they wheeled toward the office. Simon had to chuckle that his former pastime was about to become a citywide event. Instead of snatching a random brochure here and there, he was about to distribute the mother lode with the help of the Darkness. *Times sure have changed.*

Simon began opening file cabinets and grabbing folders full of propaganda. He didn't care much about staying organized or sorting through folders: everything would be tossed throughout Westbend in a matter of hours.

"Simon?" Chin said. Simon looked up to see that Chin and Malachi were standing by an open closet door. Simon walked toward them to see boxes and boxes stacked inside. A few of them were opened, and Simon smiled.

"Well, that's easier," he admitted, looking at piles of pamphlets.

The closet was emptied in no time, and while the truck's trailer was by no means full, there were plenty of nonsensical slogans and ominous threats to go around.

"People are going to understand this, right? That these pamphlets are ridiculous and should be regarded as drivel?"

Chin reached down to pick up a tract that had fallen near his foot. "Most of these look old and a bit outdated. And the genius of New Morgan's campaign was that it was deliberately incremental in the degrees of rhetoric."

"Umm, sorry. What now?"

"When proponents of New Morgan wanted to convince people to adhere to their values and discard other thinking, they had to be slow about it. Anything too drastic would have produced too much backlash. But by minimizing the reactions to a few protests by groups the government could label as extremists, and by progressively strengthening their messages and confiscating the old ones, the masses were slowly brainwashed before they realized what was happening. Here, we're tossing everything out there at the same time, intentionally telling the story in a matter of minutes. People will no doubt consult with others and compare tracts. And if nothing else, it will add to the confusion of the moment and—hopefully—encourage people to think."

"As long as they're not too afraid to think," Simon said, suddenly a little skeptical when he thought of Ben and some of his former classmates.

"Ella and her parents are evidence that some are. Maybe more people than we know."

"It is time," Malachi said, gesturing for Simon to ride in back with the boxes of government-issued rubbish.

Simon heaved a sigh. "Fine. Just don't leave me in here, all right?"

Simon wasn't certain, but he was pretty sure he saw Malachi roll his eyes as he lowered the trailer door.

To Simon's relief, the trip lasted only a few minutes. The door raised to dozens of Messengers wearing dark coats and anxious expressions. Steam rose from their lips as they breathed in the mid-January air.

"You all know what to do," Chin said quickly. "Grab some papers, distribute them where you can, and return to the City quickly so we know you are safe. If possible, send one Messenger home; the other Messenger will make the safety report for both at the South Gate. If you make it back to Grand Station, you are welcome to stay for the night if you're willing to be away from your home Saturday morning. May the Lord guard and keep us all."

In the distance, rumbling sounded, and Simon wasn't sure whether he hoped it was thunder or the sounds of battle.

Simon helped pass out stacks of pamphlets to pairs, including Charity, who was going with Zeke. Wordlessly, they exchanged looks of concern before she turned and went out into the night. When all pairs had gone, only Malachi, Chin, Ella, and Simon were left.

"The Bot's around the corner," Ella whispered. They both took large boxes and nodded good-bye to the last two Messengers, who would be using the truck.

"I wish we could take more," Ella said after they were inside the Bot. "We'll definitely be able to cover more ground than the truck. But there's not much cargo space," she lamented.

"How'd it run getting here?" Simon asked, securing the restraint around him.

Ella smiled. "Like this." And with that, Ella pressed a series of buttons, stepped on a pedal, and beamed as the Bot shot forward with such speed that Simon had to catch his breath until his instinct to shout had passed.

"G-g-good job," he finally managed, and Ella flashed a devious grin.

"Better get those papers ready. We're almost on the far side of town."

Simon was glad they had planned to take the northernmost part of Westbend; there was no way any Messengers had reached this area, so collision with a concealed Messenger was unlikely.

"I'm sure glad you know how to drive this thing," Simon said warily as he reached for a box behind him. If Ella's reaction time had been off, they would be no more than a metallic black smear on the side of a building by now. He pulled out two different pamphlets and held one stack in each hand.

"Get ready. Opening the hatch!"

The panel directly above them began to open, and Simon saw stars race past them. Simon held his hands up just above the opening and loosed his grip on the top layers of flyers. The papers flew behind them and lifted high into the air before fluttering down to the ground.

"Perfect!" Simon said exultantly and grabbed two more handfuls.

They covered ground in no time, and Simon finally realized how quiet the Bot was. "This is more like a stealth car than a Bot, Ella. I can barely hear it!"

"That was the idea," Ella said proudly.

"Well, great job."

"I just wish Spence could have been the first to drive it," she confessed, biting her lip. Simon nodded, but didn't say anything. He grabbed more New Morgan issues and tossed them into the night.

"That's it," Simon said soon after. He couldn't believe their success.

"Mission accomplished, and test drive complete," Ella answered. She decreased her speed slightly as she began making the way back to the City.

"Wait. What's that?" Simon pointed. Up ahead and to the right, there was a glow coming from an alley.

"I'll stop. They won't be able to see us," Ella said, shifting a few levers.

"Wait, I think something's up."

Silently, Ella steered the Bot closer and gasped. A Westbend Bot was facing away from Ella and Simon, framing two Messengers with its spotlight.

"We have to do something!" Simon hissed, suddenly concerned he could be heard through the still-open space above them.

Ella frowned in concentration. "Got it!" With that, she flipped on three switches and covered the Bot in glaring light.

The Westbend Bot was conic in shape, and its tip rotated until it focused on them. But it didn't move immediately.

"The paint. It really does absorb light," Ella said. "But between the lights and the reflection of the windshield, they know we're here." Ella backed up and then drove down the alley in the opposite direction of the Messengers. But she wasn't going very quickly.

"I need them to follow us," she explained.

Bang! Something hard slammed against the back of their Bot.

"They're following us, all right," Simon answered as the other Bot's light came toward them with alarming speed.

"Perfect," Ella said. She punched a few more buttons, and in a split second, they were off—flying through Westbend and leaving the Bot behind.

"Hope that gave them enough time to hide," Ella said. Simon nodded. He hadn't been able to tell who the Messengers had been.

Ella slowed down again, keeping an eye out for more trouble and lessening their chance of collision. When they reached the South Gate, Simon felt relief, dread, and exhaustion all at once. Ella drove a few blocks farther down an alley and let the motor run.

"Mind getting the door?"

Simon realized she was indicating a narrow garage door in front of them. He hopped out of the Bot and pulled on a chain on the right. The door slid up, and Ella pulled the Bot in. Simon followed behind, realizing this was the ramp positioned behind Spence's cellar.

The next moments were surreal as Simon closed the ramp door and Ella inspected the back of the Bot.

"They shot some sort of projectile at us, but I can't tell what it was," she said. "One thing's for sure. It'll take some time to fix."

Simon nodded, but his mind was far from the cellar. "Think we're the first ones back?" he asked.

"We'd have to be, I'd think. The others carried fewer papers and were closer to the gates, but they're on foot."

Simon didn't spend any more time wondering. He raced to the Room of the Martyrs, where the nine fire pits were all blazing.

"Simon! You're safe. What a joy to see you, dear. Come sit by a fire and warm yourself." Mrs. Meyer ushered Simon into the middle of the room and handed him a cup.

"Thank you, Mrs. Meyer." He wasn't very cold since he had been inside a vehicle, but there was no point in arguing with her. He took a hearty gulp of black coffee, not caring that it scalded his taste buds.

"Ah, Ella! Come in, come in . . ." Simon smiled as Mrs. Meyer rushed off to the next Messenger. He turned toward the entryway where the South Gate tunnel opened to the Room of the Martyrs. Now, it was time to wait.

Johann and another Elder were the next to arrive, and they took up position at a table near the tunnel. Simon realized they were taking on the duty of checking in the others who returned.

The next few who came in were brief: they reported that their partners had made it home, and they left to return home themselves. Ella joined Simon, and the two enjoyed the scene that the next pair of Messengers caused.

"We were done for. I just knew it," one Messenger said emphatically. Simon recognized both of them as Carriers who often took missions in the East Sector.

"But then! What was it, Rick? There was a huge light that came outta nowhere!"

"I think it was a Bot."

"Did you see a Bot, Rick?"

"Well, no."

"There was a light, and some sort of shiny thing, and that was it."

"Think it was an angel?"

"Oooh, do you think?"

Simon looked at Ella, who was pink with delight. He wasn't sure if they should explain, but he saw Johann look over at Ella and him with a smile. Johann turned back and continued talking with the pair.

The next Messenger's report came in stark contrast. A woman Simon didn't recognize rushed in, tears streaking her face.

"We were done. We were nowhere near the pamphlets anymore and were on the way home. I was. I was going to go home, and he was going to report back. So close. But we came around the corner, and . . . and . . . it was Maximalus. I recognized it right away from the Arena. And . . . and . . ." The woman was reduced to sobs, and Johann led her out of the Room of the Martyrs. Simon looked at the murals on the wall, knowing that the martyrs painted here were only a fraction of those who had lost their lives for their faith in Jesus Christ. He looked at the image of his mom, and he could empathize with the woman who came in. He pictured his father in his mind, and the sadness grew.

He felt an encouraging arm around his shoulder, and he looked over to Ella. She looked straight ahead, at his mom's image. For a few moments, Simon took comfort in the sympathy of his friend.

More people came in, and Simon's reaction was increasingly conflicted. He rejoiced at each report of safety, but his anxiety grew as he failed to see a pair of short, quick-footed Messengers. The tension grew even more when there was a lull of Messengers who came through the tunnel. Simon watched as the Elder and another Messenger, who joined the table as Johann left, began looking at their list and comparing notes. There must only be a few left.

Chin and Malachi ended the lull, and Simon was thrilled to see that they were both safe. All had been successful, and they had returned the truck to the warehouse before walking back. This explanation only heightened Simon's fear for the last missing pair: Charity and Zeke.

Malachi slowly walked up to Simon, and Simon noticed that Ella inched away a bit, almost as if he would need some space. Dread fell heavy on his entire being.

"Don't worry, Simon. They will be safe."

For a moment, Simon felt a sense of relief until panic surged again.

"Wait a minute. What kind of 'safe,' Malachi?" Simon didn't have to remind him what he'd said about Simon's father.

"Do not fear, Simon."

Simon stood up, trying in vain to keep down all the anger toward Malachi that he thought he had overcome, when he heard a small cheer near the tunnel.

"Hooray! Zeke! Charity!"

Malachi moved aside to reveal the scene behind him. A small crowd welcomed them into the room as the two at the table marked off the last two names and stood up from their chairs.

Zeke waved away the welcome as silliness. "Bah, don't mind an old man who's not as spry as he used to be." An appreciative chuckle passed around the room, and Mrs. Meyer welcomed them both with hugs and hot coffee. Simon knew better, though. Zeke was still as spry as some who were decades younger.

Charity walked up to Ella and Simon. Ella gave her a big hug and retreated, obviously leaving the two of them alone at the fire pit. Charity sat down, and Simon almost glared at her.

"We're even."

"What?"

"From your birthday night. When I almost died. Now we're even."

Charity opened her mouth, preparing an appropriate counterpoint, but she froze and thought better of it. With a smile and a shrug, she offered a sideways "Fair enough."

Simon rolled his eyes and sank down next to her, relief and exhaustion taking over now that the fear had left. His head fell into his hands, and he allowed Charity to give him a patronizingly light pat on the back.

"One mission down," she reported. "Two more to go."

Chapter Twenty-Two

The cellar had a renewed energy about it as Ella dashed around the room in a search for the best means to improve the Bot. But the space wasn't quite the same, and the effort was literally halfhearted, with one Messenger still missing.

"I just can't seem to find . . . ah, here. But what if . . . no, that's not right." Ella's fragmented conversations with herself along with the clinking of tools on metal provided the background noise for the work at hand. It was also noticeable that the sounds of a good-natured bravado were lacking.

Charity and Simon would visit when they could, but neither of them could fill the void formed by the absences of Spence and Jack.

"Baaaah! I give up!" Ella declared at one point, tossing a socket wrench into a bin. "I just can't do this," she elaborated, lying down on the floor in a demonstration of futility.

Simon and Charity were both in the room, and they exchanged glances, knowing that Ella wasn't just complaining about the mechanical project.

"Any news on the front, Ella?" Charity asked.

Ella rocked her head back and forth on the ground, answering in the negative. A tear trailed down her cheek. "And of course the news doesn't say anything I can believe. But we know war is coming. We can hear it every night. Louder each time."

"Well," Simon ventured, "the way I see it, we're running out of time then, right? I mean, if we're going to find more passages, who knows what'll happen when the battle lines reach Westbend? We might be stuck in hiding for months. Or in the blink of an eye, everything will change. I don't know about you, but we're going to have to move on to our second mission fast."

"Simon," Ella muttered, "I don't know if you've noticed, but there's a huge dent in the back of the Bot!"

"It still runs, doesn't it?"

"Yes."

"Well, I don't see a problem, then."

Ella sat up in exasperated disbelief that Simon would suggest taking a beaten-up Bot out onto the streets. Most of her hair had escaped her ponytail, creating a spectacle that reminded Simon of the sun with its wild rays circling in every angle. He bit his lip, hoping a laugh wouldn't emerge.

"He might have a point, Ella," Charity offered. "After all, we made the necessary changes already, right?"

This brought a smile from Ella, and she hopped up to her feet. Absently, she pulled her hair back and fixed the tie.

"Yes, I suppose it'll do. It's still quiet, it's still fast, and now, it has space for three."

"Three?" Simon asked.

Charity flashed a brilliant smile. "Ella added one more seat."

The added seat was little more than a ledge and a restraint squeezed in the place where the boxes had been on the Bot's first mission. Charity looked cramped in the small space, but Simon knew she wouldn't complain one bit. Simon walked up the ramp and opened the overhead door, standing guard as Ella drove the machine out of the cellar and into the alley. After securing the entrance, Simon hopped in. He barely had enough time to fasten his restraint before Ella stepped on the pedal, propelling the Bot forward at breakneck speed. Simon heard Charity gasp behind him.

In no time, the southern border of Westbend vanished from sight, and they were on the open road. The night sky provided the only light, and Simon worried that Ella might not see any obstacles on the road in time to avoid them, but it was more important to maintain stealth. He just hoped that any scarce-yet-approved vehicle that might be on the road would use lights.

"How long till we get there?" Charity asked.

"I did a little research on the Internet this week," Ella responded. "It would take a normal car a little over an hour to get there. It should take us just under an hour. Less, if I push it, but I want to be careful. I'm just not certain if there are any internal consequences from the damage in the back."

Simon smiled at the fact that this was slow in Ella's terms. He was just now getting used to the speed at which the lines on the street blurred underneath them.

"So, Charity, since we have time to chat," Simon began, "what's the real scoop behind you and Zeke being so late on our last mission? We all know the two of you have no trouble moving quickly."

Simon had been waiting for this opportunity. Charity couldn't get away, and with Ella around, it would seem less like a confrontation and more like a conversation. Still, Simon's concern for Charity wouldn't let him shake the mystery behind that night.

Charity waited a moment before beginning.

"Things went smoothly, for the most part. We delivered the pamphlets without any trouble, and we were on our way back from the East Sector. Suddenly, though, a flashlight came on in the middle of an alley when we walked past, and a Security guard stood there with a big smile on his face. He was proud of himself for thinking to hide and wait. Then another flashlight came on, and a second Security guard appeared behind us. We were trapped."

Even though Charity was right there in the Bot, Simon's throat tightened. He knew she was safe now, but the thought of Charity in the clutches of New Morgan again made him feel ill.

"But then Zeke did what Zeke does best. I have no idea how he does it. He somehow convinces them that he's no threat at all. And he tells this crazy, convoluted story about why we're out in the middle of the night, that even I can't follow it anymore. He's my grandpa; I was looking for something. . . . They're confused and a little bit annoyed, but somehow intrigued by this little guy with crazy hair who's not afraid of them one bit!"

Charity's voice danced with a hint of laughter, marveling at the skills of Westbend's oldest Elder.

"Then, right as they're about to decide what to do with us, a truck drives past. Maybe it was Chin and Malachi. I dunno. Either way, it distracted the guards. 'Ah!' Zeke says, 'Aha! There they are. Didn't I just say we were waiting for that truck?! Well, then. Good night, gentlemen! And do keep safe, won't you?'" Charity's impression of Zeke was uncanny, and Simon couldn't help but smile despite his lingering worry.

"Of course, Zeke said nothing about a truck before, but the Security guards were so confused by that point that they had no idea what to do. They just mildly nodded and watched as Zeke calmly escorted me away. I just don't know how he does it," Charity added. "It's like the time he rescued me from the slave owner. He acts like he has no worry in the world, and it baffles everyone into listening to him."

Simon had always liked Zeke, and he'd always known that Zeke and Charity had a special relationship. But he was more thankful than ever that Charity's "grandpa" happened to be the smartest Messenger in Westbend.

For a time, the three fell silent as they approached their next task: unearth illegal documents from under a pile of rubble in a small, unfamiliar town. Eventually, Ella broke the silence.

"So, what exactly is the plan here?" Ella asked.

"This would have been a good time for Ben to have done some research at the library for us," Simon admitted. His nagging frustration with Ben's absence rose to the surface again. "All I know is that there had been a seminary. And it's nothing but rubble now. I'm hoping we can somehow figure out where it was and dig around. For Ella's sake, we need to get back before the morning. But if we don't get far tonight, maybe we can try again soon."

"Ugh," Ella groaned. "I know it's a stretch, but I sure hope we don't have to come more than once."

Conversation fell silent as they drew near a town smaller than any Simon had ever seen. A few dim street lamps helped Simon estimate that two dozen or so homes huddled in a small square of lots surrounding the main road. A few other buildings on the main street were either tired and worn or completely boarded up. The dark windows of a market were lined with signs announcing what produce was currently out of stock. Simon's old sense of nostalgia for forgotten buildings came back. He could imagine the town in a brighter era, with freshly painted storefronts and new awnings. A small tavern appeared to be operational, even though it was closed at this time of night.

A particularly haunting building tugged at Simon as he stared up at its boarded windows and tall, crumbling tower. The tower had large archways at the top, and Simon wondered what used to be the purpose of this structure. There appeared to be some sort of ornament on top that had been broken off, its jagged base the only reminder. Simon remembered the hymn about steeples falling, and he realized he must be looking at one.

"I'm not sure, but I think this must have been a church," Simon suggested.

New Morgan hadn't bothered to cover up these hollow buildings with plaster facades. Instead, these skeletal structures stared blankly at the residents who still lived here.

Ella drove down the main street slowly, and Simon noticed that her hands were clenched around the wheel. Just a minute or two out of town, they approached a road that passed between two dilapidated columns to nowhere in particular.

"I have a hunch that we've found it," Simon said, pointing to the forlorn gateway. He was both relieved that they had found it so quickly and apprehensive to visit the site of such tragedy. Also, without the cover of shelter, the three would have a difficult time hiding once they left their discreet vehicle.

Ella veered right and took the road to the top of a hill, where the pavement ended. The three climbed out and were silent, taking in the void. Sidewalks were half buried under overgrowth, but they could tell the overall layout of the campus by the way the walkways stretched out from a central location.

Charity walked to a stone outline of a former build-ing. Wrought iron twisted and stretched out like dead beetles with wiry legs to the sky. She knelt near one of the metallic carcasses and picked up a shard of something from the ground.

"Colored glass," she announced.

"I wonder if this was the chapel," Ella replied.

Charity walked around its perimeter, kicking up debris and occasionally picking up pieces of pottery, stone, or glass.

Simon headed to the heart of the walkways, where the concrete formed a circle. A shallow basin evidenced that this had been a fountain or pond of some sort. Now, it contained foul, stagnant water, mud, and rotting leaves.

He moved past to one of the largest perimeters he saw. Remnants of brick and stone littered the area, and Simon walked straight into the middle of the former building. Grass and mud covered construction debris. It looked as if a giant child had knocked down his playthings and left them to decay for years. He kicked over a stone, hoping to find some clue of the building's former life.

He noticed remnants of a splintered desk, and he crouched to see if anything was left in a drawer. The only drawer that remained was unrelenting in staying shut. Either it was locked, or it was cemented with age. Simon wondered if he could find an ax or a—

"Aaaaaah!" Simon was too panicked to withhold a shout. The ground beneath him gave way, and he crashed down, tumbling until he landed several feet below the surface.

"Simon!" Charity shouted. Both Ella and Charity ran toward him, but stopped before careening into the gaping hole.

Simon wanted to yell with the intense pain he felt in his leg, but his fear of being discovered kept him gasping for breath instead of making more noise. When his vision began to clear, he saw that he had fallen down an old staircase and into an open basement. What he found left him speechless.

"Simon?" Charity asked.

"Simon? Are you okay?" Ella added.

"Simon! Answer me!" Charity demanded with desperation.

Simon answered by popping his head out of the hole, causing both of his counterparts to scream.

"Sorry," he said, but he was beaming. He climbed gingerly up the stairs, favoring his injured leg. "But look what I found."

Chapter Twenty-Three

He closed the door behind him. He knew his colleagues would start to wonder about his frequent trips away from campus, but what choice did he have? They would only believe he had to visit his mother so often. Little did they know how precariously her power hung in the balance. That she would repeatedly threaten the life of her son or grandson—either one, it didn't matter much to her. The loyal subject his entire life long, or the outlaw child of her rebel daughter. She was desperate.

The rampant infractions of the Darkness clearly showed the ineffectual precautions his mother had taken. If only she'd listen to his advice . . . Not that he was without concerns of his own. It was maddening that his own nephew would turn away from his teachings. And to make things worse, the boy and his accomplices were giving other rebels hope. He saw it in their eyes. They didn't cower anymore. They no longer felt alone. Of all the nerve, they actually tried to convince him that he was wrong! Every stunt the Darkness pulled only encouraged the others.

One thing was certain. With or without his mother's help, Simon Clay would pay.

Simon climbed out of the hole slowly, testing each stair step before he put his weight on it. He held out his hand and produced a small book, torn in half. Ella pulled out a flashlight and focused it on the book as Simon turned a few pages. The letters looked nothing like their alphabet, but as he turned a few pages, he knew he had seen many of these letters before as a Carrier. When the message was pending.

"Look, I see a γ and a ς and a λ. This is Greek. It could be more of the λόγος."

Ella and Charity stared in disbelief.

"You were right, Simon. You did it."

"And by falling into a hole!"

"Quick," Simon urged, "let's get this to the Bot. Then, maybe we can go back down there and find more. I saw shelves . . ."

Ella nodded and snatched the book. She ran to the Bot, placing the Message out of sight.

Simon turned and looked down at the stairs, but a rock moved under his foot, and he winced in pain.

"Simon!" Charity scolded. "You're hurt again."

"I'll be okay. If I could just—"

"Simon, that floor collapsed. What's to say it won't collapse again—this time with you underneath?"

Simon tried to move forward, but he fell to the ground, hitting his right knee on a long piece of metal. Blood dripped from the jagged cut, and Simon groaned in disgust. If only he could rely on his body to get where he needed to go . . .

"Here. I'll see if I can find a stick or something for a crutch. Take this for a bandage." From her pocket, Charity pulled out a handkerchief she sometimes used in her hair when she painted. Then, she dashed off to find some sort of help for Simon as he wrapped the cloth around his knee.

Seconds later, Simon's heart stopped at a bloodcurdling scream. The scream came from Ella, who had started to walk back to Simon. But she was staring to Simon's right.

There. Simon's blood turned cold as he turned to see. Charity stood perfectly still, her face blank and smooth as glass. Behind her, Roderick Druck stood with one hand gripping her upper arm, a blade pressed against her neck.

"Ah, Nephew. We meet again at last. You wouldn't believe the measures I've taken to find you. I've visited your apartment. Quaint little dwelling. I've had chats with your friends, Spence and Cyril. Pity, they've been no help at all. And I've even come here—I knew this would be the place I would find you. My mother thought I was a fool, but what does she know? It seems I figured it out even before you did." Roderick's cloying laugh pierced the air.

"Ah, to see her face now as I have you in my grip." He squeezed Charity's arm until she winced, and Simon clenched his fists.

"Hello, Uncle." Simon forced every nerve in his body to calm down enough for his voice to sound even and cool. "What is it that you want from me?"

Roderick's teeth gleamed in the night as he flashed a garish smile.

"Oh, don't you know? My dear Simon, let me tell you a little secret." Druck walked a few steps closer, pushing Charity roughly along. The knife threatened with every move, but it did not strike her skin.

"My mother, you see. She's decided to create a little game. Remember the night your friend Micah met his untimely end? Well, that was a special night for the two of us. Your grandmother has decided that on the anniversary of that night, one of us will be dead. It's a little competition, don't you see? So. For the past several months, it's been difficult to play our game when I can't find you anywhere. I'd like to change that tonight, Simon. From now on, I want to know where you are. Every. Single. Day."

Simon stared at Charity. He marveled at her ability to appear calm, but he knew better. Even in the darkness, he could see her green eyes, and he knew they were terrified.

"Well, Druck," Simon said, praying he appeared strong and confident, "how can we make that happen for you?"

"Ah, good lad. This girl. She's very valuable, you know." He raised up her arm. "She's a slave, and this brand happens to indicate that she belongs to me. I have many employees, and I would love to discover which one let this little gem escape."

"I was paid for," Charity spat. But Simon's stomach only churned. Druck ignored her.

"And she's growing up into a lovely little thing, I might add. You can imagine that she's much more valuable now than ever before."

It took every fiber of Simon's being to keep from lunging at Druck and strangling him with his bare hands. But the knife—it was so close to Charity's neck.

"Now, I'm willing to make a little deal with you, Simon. You come toward me, slowly. And I'll let my slave girl free. She can run off with your friend over there," he said, nodding to Ella. "A fair trade, no?"

Charity's mask broke, and tears streamed down her face. Simon couldn't bear the sight, and he agonized over what he was putting her through. They both knew that her birthday, the anniversary of Micah's death, could possibly be his last day on earth. Simon gradually raised his hands and walked toward Druck. Pain shot through his leg, but it was no comparison to the misery he was enduring for Charity's sake. When Simon was a few steps away, Druck brandished a pair of handcuffs and tossed them his way.

"Now. One on your wrist and one on mine. That's it."

When Simon was linked to his uncle, Roderick shoved Charity to the ground. She kicked his knee so hard, Simon thought he heard a crack. Druck screamed in anger.

"Insolent wretch! You fool! You've just cost your friend here more pain than you want to know."

Charity's eyes grew large in fear as she scrambled to her feet. Without hesitation, Simon shouted, praying that she would listen.

"Charity! Run!"

She did, and Ella grabbed her and pulled her toward the Bot.

"What in the world?!"

Simon realized with satisfaction that Druck hadn't seen the Bot with its ultra-dark paint. In a matter of seconds, the two Messengers vanished into the vehicle, which sped away silently into the night.

"Enjoy this moment, Simon," Druck hissed. "It's the last time you'll see either of them again."

With that, Simon felt a sharp stabbing pain in his thigh. Everything went dark.

Chapter Twenty-Four

Before Simon opened his eyes, he knew where he was. The details might be different, but he'd been in enough prison cells to know what one felt like. The stone dungeon below Druck-Baden Manor. The sterile cell in the Arena. The dark room high up in City Hall. He opened his eyes.

And now here. Wherever this was. The room was incredibly small. The cot he was lying on covered the entire length of the back wall. The room was square, its only other furnishing a metal toilet and a rectangular hole in the wall, which appeared to be covered with a metal flap. He guessed this was the means for meal delivery. Smooth beige tiles lined the walls, which only rose high enough that Simon could touch the plaster ceiling if he stood and held his hands up. The floor was covered with small hexagon tiles that had probably been white under the layer of grime. The metal door finished the job in keeping him completely shut out from the outside world. A round, white fixture overhead cast the room in a yellowish light.

Simon lay still, collecting his thoughts. This would be the kind of place one could go mad, but he wasn't about to lose his wits to Roderick Druck. Again.

He gingerly lifted his left leg, and a dull ache warned him not to try moving it any more. He lifted his right knee to inspect his wound. It had stopped bleeding, thanks to Charity's handkerchief. Charity. Simon touched the fabric, and tears welled in his eyes. He might never see her again. Right now, she would know he was in danger, and she would know that with each day, time was running out. But at least he knew she was safe. For now, that was enough.

He thought back to the last time he saw her face and the fear that marked her expression. Over the past few months, he'd been so proud of her for letting her guard down, for opening up, and for trusting others. Now, he felt that he'd betrayed her in that transformation. Now, her shield was down, and he was responsible for wounding her deeper than he could have imagined.

"Keep your distance, Simon."

Simon heard her voice echo in his mind as he pictured the two of them in the Arena, talking as if they were the only people in the world. She had warned him. There was no doubt he was better for knowing her, but was she better off? Guilt flooded in. She had insisted that she'd be trouble for him, but it was the other way around.

A strangled moan escaped his lips, which must have been loud enough to reach the hallway outside.

"Simon? Are you awake? I do hope you rested well. I feel it necessary to offer one note of caution. My mother, you see, does not know where you are. You are quite safe from her at the moment."

Simon rolled his eyes at the poor excuse for comfort.

"But I'm no fool. You see, you are hiding right under her nose. So if you shout or make any loud noises, she'll no doubt come down to see what the trouble is. And what will she find? You."

Druck's low laugh sounded more annoying than threatening, but Simon didn't have the energy to respond. Now, he knew where he was: City Hall, probably right under the room where he had confronted his grandmother and Micah. He mused how many holding cells must be in this building; this one was nothing like the one that overlooked the town, the one he had escaped with his uncle's help the last time he was here.

"I'll be visiting you later today, my dear nephew. Until then."

Simon fell asleep again; there was no use fighting his exhaustion and whatever was still coursing through his veins after his uncle's injection at the seminary ruins. He would need to steel himself against whatever was to come next. When he woke again, he felt a little better. It was time to gain strength in other ways as well. Food was waiting for him in the wall slot. He knew it could be poisoned, but he didn't have much choice. He ate small bites of the dry bread and drank some of the water.

He passed over the cold piece of beef, which had more gristle than meat.

He savored the next moments of quiet; it was time to pray. He prayed for Charity and Ella. For Jack. For Zeke and Johann and Chin. For his grandparents. He prayed for Spence and Cyril and wondered for a moment how close they might be. And then, without even planning it, he even prayed for his uncle Roderick. After all, without knowing the God who listens, he didn't have a prayer.

With deliberate care, he slowly stretched his muscles: his neck, shoulders, arms . . . then eventually his legs. When his left leg began to throb, he gently massaged his muscles to loosen them up. He bent his legs so that his head rested on his knees. A familiar scent surprised him, and he realized he'd caught the fragrance of the handkerchief around his right knee. He knew that smell well: He'd smelled it in the Arena when he collided with Charity for the first time. He'd smelled it in the City, a fragrance both new and familiar. It was the scent of Grand Station, of home and those he loved.

He began his next exercise. *In Him was life, and the life was the light of men. The light shines in the darkness, and the darkness has not overcome it.* He thought of John and all he went through, and was moved at the poetry the disciple was still able to write. *Though I walk through the valley of the shadow of death, I will fear no evil, for You are with me.* Simon remembered how often he took comfort from Psalm 23 the other times he had faced Roderick Druck.

Simon thought next of Jack and the battles his friend was facing right now. He remembered a passage from Romans that Jack had shared in the truck. *For I consider that the sufferings of this present time are not worth comparing with the glory that is to be revealed to us.* And he remembered the psalm that seemed so pertinent to his life during worship, one that only grew in significance now. *Attend to my cry, for I am brought very low! Deliver me from my persecutors, for they are too strong for me! Bring me out of prison, that I may give thanks to Your name!*

It was time. Simon allowed his mind to venture into a place he rarely dared to go: the memory that eventually triggered his revelation that he had, in fact, forsaken the Word, his father, and his God. He pictured the night when he had woken up, sweating and sick to his stomach. The dream, he had known, was more than a dream. It was a memory of the past he wanted to forget. And why? Because Simon had lost that night to Mr. Druck, the phantom who haunted his dreams and now demanded a place in reality as well.

Simon closed his eyes and relived the memory. He remembered his uncle's confident smile. He remembered the table spinning him around, leaving him completely disoriented. But the worst part of the memory happened even before Druck opened his mouth. He remembered his thoughts: that he was smarter than Druck. That he could handle it—alone. *Give me your worst*, Simon had silently dared his uncle. And his uncle had. "Well, Mr. Clay," he had said. "It seems you're just too smart for all of this."

Simon swallowed hard as now he saw that the words had been his uncle's declaration of victory. He had seen something in Simon that night that signaled the end of his work. Whether he realized it or not, Druck had seen pride. Self-righteousness. And a total lack of trust in God.

Jack's voice came back to Simon's mind, quoting words from John. *In the world you will have tribulation. But take heart; I have overcome the world.* These words from Jesus put Simon's heart at ease. With the help of God, he was ready.

The lock clicked, and the door opened. Roderick Druck stepped inside and brought in a small folding chair.

"Ah, Simon. It's such a pleasure to welcome you to your new home. Let's begin by catching up, shall we?"

Simon saw the look of horror on his uncle's face when he smiled. "Uncle Roderick, it would be my pleasure."

Chapter Twenty-Five

Isolated. Captured. Banished. I am all alone. Who could have known that my life would come to this? A quarrelsome fisherman is somehow recruited by the very Son of God to walk the earth with Him and witness to His deeds. The Word became flesh and dwelt among me. And now, the Word is in me. I have seen so much darkness in this world, and much of it came from within me! But the Light of light now shines through me, that I may shine the truth to others.

Yes, I am alone, separated from those whom I love— my children—dear fellow believers who look to me for the Word of truth. And yet, I am not alone. For our Lord and Savior promised to be with us all until He returns. And for me, it is enough to bear witness, to testify to the truth, that others may believe and have life.

■ ■ ■

Simon was exhausted. His left leg was swollen and felt warm, and he used most of his strength to prop it up against his other foot. He couldn't remember half of what he had said to Druck, but he prayed that his words would work on him. He thought of his father. Sorrow washed over him, but he no longer felt anger. He no longer felt the overwhelming urge to hide in a cloud of numbing denial and burning hate. He could still feel those shadows threaten on his periphery, but they were not as powerful as they once were.

"Forgive . . . forgive them, Simon." Simon could hear the words of his father, and tears came to his eyes. Roderick Druck killed his father. If it was a mistake, it was only because Simon was the true target. Simon knew that if there was someone he had reason to hate . . . it would be his uncle. For hating his mother. For enslaving Charity. For torturing him. For killing his father. And the list continued to grow.

"Forgive . . ."

Simon had refused these words at first, but that had only hurt him. He remembered his father's own explanation behind forgiveness: "'I can do all things through Him who strengthens me.'"

He heard a low rumble, and he knew that it must be nightfall. The sounds of battle carried across the night air.

A haunting tune that Simon had never heard before drifted toward him and lulled him with a strong, steady melody. He could not recognize the language, but he thought he recognized the voice.

"Cyril?"

"Yes, Simon. It is me."

Simon felt a wave of joy to hear Cyril's voice and to know he was not completely alone.

"It is safe to talk at night, Simon. Everyone has gone home."

Simon didn't know that he trusted his grandma to be reliable about anything, but he trusted Cyril for knowing this place. And the happiness that came with talking to a fellow believer overcame his fears of being caught.

"Cyril, we've missed you! Have you been here all this time? It's been more than three months!"

"Yes, Simon. It has been a very long time."

"Cyril?" Simon felt trepidation creep up his spine. He didn't want to ask the question on his lips. "Is Spence here too?"

A moment of silence confirmed Simon's worst fear.

"He was here, yes. Now, he is with the Lord."

All-new sorrow, all-new grief. Simon wondered if there would ever be a time he would not have to face the constant threat of mourning and loss.

"Druck did it, didn't he?"

"He began the questioning when we first arrived. But his questions were strange, Simon. To be sure, he asked about the Messengers and where they hide. He asked especially about you and where you lived. But there were other questions too. He would ridicule our faith, but the questions he asked almost opened doors to the Gospel. It was as if he secretly wanted to learn more about the Word."

Simon couldn't believe it. And yet, if his grandma balanced Roderick's life against his own, why was Simon still alive? Why didn't his uncle just bring Simon to greet his grandmother—and his death?

"Over time, his mother grew impatient with the time it took Roderick to get answers from us. She began to question us herself, and she used torture."

Simon thought back to his nights in the Druck-Baden Manor. Had Mr. Druck, headmaster, actually learned his techniques from his own mother?

"Spence was fearless. She asked about moles in the government, about traitors in the military, about our headquarters, about you. But Spence said nothing."

Simon thought about the Maxons and about Jack. Spence had protected them all.

"In the end, it was complications from his wounds, based on what he described to me at night. I've been alone for a month now."

"I'm so sorry."

After some time, Cyril began humming the tune again.

"Cyril? What are you singing?"

"It is a song that we sang from where I grew up. Here are some of the words: 'For me You gave all Your love, For me You suffered pain; I find no words, nothing can Your selflessness explain. What kind of love is this? What kind of love is this? You showed Your love, Jesus, there To me on Calvary.'"

It was strange, but Simon drew great comfort knowing that Jesus, God Himself, knew pain and sorrow as well. He drew the greatest comfort from knowing that Jesus endured it all willingly out of love for him.

"Cyril," Simon asked, "do you think other believers are in prison tonight too? That others are going through trials like this?"

"Most certainly," came the reply. "Many countries near my homeland experienced war, violence, and even persecution. It is one reason why I came to Morganland. In order to study the Word, I needed to come to a place of peace."

Simon didn't hold back a raw, bitter laugh. "Well, Cyril, we failed you there. I'm sorry you came from one struggle to the next."

"Someday, I will know peace. In that, I have great hope."

Before long, Simon began to drift off to sleep, listening to the rich sound of Cyril's song, punctuated by the growing sounds of war.

Chapter Twenty-Six

There was no mistaking it: the war was upon them. Even from the bowels of the City Hall building, Simon could hear the explosions and feel the building tremble. Dust and debris from the ceiling would sprinkle down on him as he lay on his bed, waiting.

He felt helpless, unable to protect the City, unable to comfort his friends. His shin continued to throb. He longed for simple things: a way to elevate his leg, a cool compress, a straight stick to keep it still. Each time he raised his pant leg to examine it, his skin would be a new color. Purple, green, black.

He began to notice other bruises he had ignored while paying attention to his injured legs. Between the pain of his leg and the adrenaline of the night, he hadn't stopped to consider how injured he truly was.

His right knee had stopped bleeding. He had taken some of his water to clean the area, but he wished he was able to clean the handkerchief itself. He felt miserable that he had ruined one more thing of Charity's with his blood.

Charity. Of all Simon's injuries, his heart ached the most. His gut was twisted in concern for his family in the City: Mrs. Meyer, Ella, Zeke, Chin, but most of all, Charity. He wondered if she regretted letting him into her life. He wondered where she was, what she was doing. He prayed she wasn't doing anything to put herself in danger.

There was something strange about this prison stay. Every other time, he had assumed he was getting out. There wasn't a logical explanation about it, but his mind had been continually focused on the "what next" beyond the cell. This time, Simon didn't assume that was the case. If his grandmother found him, he would die. If Druck became impatient with him, he would die. If Revemond's army came and leveled City Hall, he would die. If the city of Westbend evacuated and he was left locked in this room with no food, he would die. There were far too many reasons why he should not expect release.

But there was something else strange about this stay as well: he felt at peace. He thought of John, who had been captured and left on an isolated island. He thought of Peter and Mark, who had suffered much for being Messengers of the truth. He thought of Paul, who had gone through nearly every trial for the sake of the λόγος and who had been imprisoned repeatedly. Words from his Letter to the Philippians went through Simon's mind: *Christ will be honored in my body, whether by life or by death. For to me to live is Christ, and to die is gain.*

Simon thought of the questions his dad used to ask him:

And what did you learn? He learned that "God so loved the world, that He gave His only Son, that whoever believes in Him should not perish but have eternal life."

Was it worth the trouble? Simon's memory came to the passage he and Jack had found in the catacombs. "For I consider that the sufferings of this present time are not worth comparing with the glory that is to be revealed to us."

What is there to lose? He thought of Paul's response: "I count everything as loss because of the surpassing worth of knowing Christ Jesus my Lord. For His sake I have suffered the loss of all things and count them as rubbish, in order that I may gain Christ."

The door opened, and Druck appeared.

"Good morning, Simon," he said, setting his chair inside and closing the door behind him. "Are you ready to continue our little game?"

Simon took a deep breath and admitted what they both knew. "Roderick Druck, if you wanted me to die, I wouldn't be here now. I would have died in the Arena, before the trial even started. Or last June, when you unlocked my cell door. Or at the seminary ruins the other night. Let's be honest, Uncle. You don't want my death. You want answers."

Chapter Twenty-Seven

"You did well, Simon," Cyril's voice echoed.

Simon, again, was completely drained. Between the energy it was taking his body to heal and the energy it was taking his mind to stay focused when talking with his uncle, he felt more tired than ever before. He had been surprised that Druck had not used any torture or drugs, as he had done in the past, but Simon doubted it would have made much difference. Every ounce of his energy was sapped, and anything more would have just made him unconscious.

"I just don't know if I can keep doing this," Simon admitted.

"You're not doing it alone. Know that I am praying for you every minute, and I am here, listening."

Simon smiled. He thanked God that he had the support of an Elder so close.

"And do not forget Jesus' words when He ascended: 'And behold, I am with you always, to the end of the age.'"

"I don't know about you, Cyril, but I'm looking forward to the end of the age more and more."

"Amen. Come, Lord Jesus."

"Hey, that's what Chin said a few months ago."

"It comes from the Book of Revelation, the last book of the Bible."

"Zeke mentioned it before, but he said we don't have it right now," Simon recalled. "Tell me more."

"When John was exiled to Patmos, he received a prophecy from the Lord. 'The revelation of Jesus Christ, which God gave Him to show to His servants the things that must soon take place. He made it known by sending His angel to His servant John.' That's the first verse."

"So an angel revealed to John a prophecy. What is it?"

"It tells of the end times: the times we live in, the times before Jesus returns. It also tells of Jesus' return and of life everlasting."

"What does it say about the end times?"

"That there will be wars, that things will be difficult for believers, that the devil will do all he can to battle against the Church."

"Tell me about it," Simon muttered. "Seems like this revelation wasn't so great."

"That's the nature of revelations. We see truth. But just as the sun blinds those accustomed to the darkness, the truth can be jarring. There is the reality of evil and sorrow. But there is also the reality of beauty, glory, and great joy. As painful as it is to be exposed to the light of truth, it nevertheless shines on eternal treasures as well."

Simon's eyes had been opened over the past eighteen months. What he learned had changed his life—for the better, without a doubt—forever. But he had also seen the horrible trouble that can come when fogs lift and shadows fade away. He'd gained so many friends, but he'd lost many too.

"You know," Simon confessed, "the more I think about it, about Micah, and Ben, and Spence . . . I realize something about fighting. Fighting really isn't so much about brother against brother. It's good against evil. Every fight we let get in the way of sharing the Message is a win for the devil. When there's conflict and we realize that the common enemy is the devil, it changes the strategy to end the conflict. Satan loses when we reconcile."

"Simon, your father would be very proud of you. I know I am."

The walls were shaking. Every few minutes, a new explosion would rock City Hall, and Simon gripped his cot, hoping to avoid another fall. He had been in the cell for a week, and he was starting to feel a little better. But he was wary of anything that could cause more problems, such as a falling tile, a collapsing cot . . .

The door slammed open. Druck's face was bright red, and his eyes were wild.

"How could you—why would you—tell me where they are!"

Simon propped himself up on his elbows and stared at Druck. "What are you talking about?"

"They did it again! You—they—why won't you just give up?! Why don't you just crawl into your holes and die?! All around us, explosions. People are fleeing. Others are looting. And you—you—you rodents are still scurrying in the streets! Everywhere I look, a message. This corner, a message. That corner, a message. The entire city of Westbend is covered in your worthless Message!"

Simon laughed. He didn't care what Druck would do in this temper; he couldn't help but chuckle.

"Why do you waste your time? Why is it so important for you to make sure everyone knows that you believe in something that the government has long ago dismissed?!"

"Uncle Roderick. If you know you have the best news in the world, and that by sharing it, you're making every single life better, why wouldn't you share it? 'We love because He first loved us.'"

"But why bother? Why not keep it to yourselves? Abigail—she was relentless, annoying, exhausting—she never stopped trying to get me to listen to her. Why waste your time on your enemies?" His eyes looked about wildly, exasperated.

Simon flashed a brilliant smile at his uncle. "Roderick Druck, people aren't the enemy. They're the prize."

Chapter Twenty-Eight

Roderick Druck opened the door without warning. He knew before he opened it what he would see: Louise Baden-Druck, frantically barking orders to her two stooges. They scrambled around the room, grabbing files and belongings.

BOOOOOOOOOOOM.

Roderick's ears rang with the closest explosion yet. The guards both fell to the ground. His mother braced herself against the heavy table. Roderick watched it all and laughed.

"Roderick! There you are. Why are you laughing like an idiot? Now, make yourself useful. Grab the files from behind you and burn them. Tell all Security to kill any prisoners we still have. I'll be in Centra by the evening. You patrol Westbend today; don't mind Revemond's troops. They'll ignore you. Take note of anything that their explosions uncover: books, criminals, hidden refuges for the undesirables. Capture who you can—don't forget, you have four months left before you bring Simon to me. Then find me tomorrow and report everything. There is no way I'm going to let this skirmish bring me down from the place I deserve. Grapner, Sprigon, go downstairs . . ."

Roderick didn't hear the rest. He turned around and walked out.

Down, down he went, taking the stairs only a few knew existed. Down to the hallway where beige tiles and closed doors concealed many secrets. It wasn't so different from the lower lair of Druck-Baden Manor, really. He stopped for a moment, picturing all the faces. Young boys and girls, waiting for whatever he might do. Trapped in dungeons to face their fate. Years and years of them. Just feet away, one such boy had waited behind a locked door. Only now, he was a young man. He'd withstood all Roderick could do or say. He'd have to kill him to silence him, but Druck would never change Simon's mind.

He stared at the door. Another explosion slammed, and pieces of plaster fell from the ceiling. He pulled out his key and turned the lock. With that, he walked away, leaving the door open.

For a moment, Simon thought the explosion had forced the door ajar, but his eye caught a flash of movement. And there, in the knob, the key glittered in the light. Simon scrambled to the door, crawling and trying not to reopen his healing wound. He snatched the keys and crawled to the next door down.

"Simon?"

"Cyril! Let's go."

Another explosion pounded, and Simon was sure the building had been hit. Tiles began to fall, and he thought he could feel the foundation underneath begin to give way. Cyril ran out and grabbed the keys. He opened every door in the hallway, but the others were empty.

"Uh, Cyril? I hate to ask this, but . . ."

Cyril reached down and pulled Simon up, supporting him on his left side.

"Quickly, now," Cyril urged. "We don't have much time."

They turned a corner and walked down the center of the building. Turning left, they walked until they found stairs. Simon hoped his adrenaline would help him as they climbed. Simon gasped as they hurried up the stairs.

"Look! An exit!" Simon couldn't help but notice a sense of déjà vu as they reached the door. Cyril pushed against it, and they both shielded their eyes as the sun's rays poured through the opening. They rushed out as the door slammed behind them. Simon couldn't believe it. He was staring at the loading dock, where he had said good-bye to Micah.

A truck honked as it rolled into the lot. Simon beamed when he saw Malachi in the driver's seat and Chin rushing out to help.

"Never fails," Simon marveled, shaking his head.

Chin and Cyril picked Simon up and laid him in the back of the trailer. Cyril sat beside him, and Chin ran back to the cabin before the engine revved and they sped away.

Simon watched buildings fly behind them as the truck drove away from City Hall with violent force. Heat, light, and a deafening noise suddenly jolted the truck, and Simon cried out as he braced himself against falling out of the open door. Cyril clung to him, keeping him inside. There was no doubt: they had just escaped the closest explosion yet. The truck turned a corner and zagged through alleyways before gradually slowing down. It turned again and traveled down a main street.

Simon sat up and took everything in as Westbend passed behind them slowly. It was surreal: it was the first time Simon had seen daylight since his father died. New Morgan lay exposed as building after building was torn apart from the battle. One building completely lost its plaster facade, and a painted sign on the now-visible brick storefront proclaimed "Kaufman's Musical Instruments." Another building suffered a gaping hole in its corner, exposing dozens of computers collecting dust on forgotten desks. Birds began to chirp, and it was only then that Simon realized there were no more explosions.

He heard the *stomp*, *stomp*, *stomp* of boots, and six soldiers wearing fatigues with the gold and red stripes of Revemond rounded the corner, marching toward them. Shadows passed over their faces as small clouds lazily drifted across the sky.

"You there! Are you a casualty?"

"Not of the war," Simon admitted.

"Are you a soldier?"

"Not of this world," Simon said with a smile. Cyril hit Simon's arm and rolled his eyes. Simon took the hint that humor might not be the best approach when conversing with an occupying army.

The soldier ignored his comment.

"There will be first-aid tents up by tonight. You will be able to receive care if you need it."

"Thank you," Simon said sincerely. He wondered if it was common protocol to have a normal conversation with an enemy of the state. Then again, he was an enemy of the state too. "Say, you don't happen to know a Caleb and Jane Clay, do you? From Maple County?"

The soldier shook his head. "Doesn't sound familiar, but I live just north of Maple County. Nice place."

"One more thing." Simon couldn't help but ask. "This might sound a little funny, but do you happen to have a Bible with you?"

"A Bible? What would you need a Bible for?"

The other soldiers laughed, and Simon couldn't decide how to react. He just laid his head back down on the trailer floor and looked up at Cyril.

"We have much work to do," the Elder answered. His face was not one of surprise but of weariness. Still, Cyril's voice held a note of resolve.

Simon watched the rooftops change against the sky as the truck continued to drive.

"Simon! Look!" Cyril pointed to the ground, and Simon sat up. On the pavement, moving slowly away from them, the Message blazed in red letters, in a handwriting he recognized.

IF ANYONE TAKES AWAY FROM THE WORDS OF THE BOOK OF THIS PROPHECY, GOD WILL TAKE AWAY HIS SHARE IN THE TREE OF LIFE AND IN THE HOLY CITY, WHICH ARE DESCRIBED IN THIS BOOK. HE WHO TESTIFIES TO THESE THINGS SAYS, "SURELY, I AM COMING SOON." AMEN. COME, LORD JESUS!

REVELATION 22:19–20

Simon whooped with joy. "We must have found the Book of Revelation!"

Cyril looked at Simon, puzzled.

Simon shook his head. "I'll explain later." He watched the words fade behind them, waiting for the next passersby.

Chapter Twenty-Nine

Simon couldn't believe his eyes. They had stopped to examine the destruction of a hollow building. The entire front wall was caved in, and an enormous hole opened in the ground. Smoke and shrapnel marked the point of impact, damaging the last few pews of the chapel below.

Malachi helped Simon walk around the perimeter.

"Be careful not to fall in," Chin warned Simon, who nodded grimly.

Simon faced the altar now and saw that the Lamb of God image was still intact. A trail of dust fell like a thin waterfall from a crack above, from an archway to the front of the center aisle. Sunlight showered the chapel floor, and the tiles glimmered in a way that Simon had never noticed before.

"Is this the only damage to the City?" Simon asked. No one answered, and Simon took a deep breath, preparing himself for what scenes could await him. He thought of the monumental impact that nearly reached them as they escaped City Hall in the truck, and he wondered how many had not made it out alive.

Back in the truck, they turned toward City Hall again. It was the last place Simon wanted to go, but it was close to the North Gate. Simon gasped when he saw that half of the government building was gone. There's no doubt that he and Cyril would have been killed in the attack, trapped in their cells as the walls caved in. But what came next shook Simon to his core. The North Gate was completely destroyed. A cavernous opening gaped wide for all to see the main entrance of Grand Station. By now, anyone in Westbend who paid attention knew that an underground group truly existed. Today, they would know where the headquarters were located. From the street, anyone could see the tunnel that led straight to the Room of the Twelve.

"Charity."

As if on cue, Simon saw her racing up the tunnel.

"Simon!" She leaped into the truck trailer and threw her arms around his neck. Simon ignored the searing pain in his leg and held her tight. Cyril hopped off the truck, inspecting the damage to the building. Charity helped Simon up, and the two sat together on the edge of the truck. Simon took Charity's hand and marveled that someone like her would face this new day together with him. Charity looked at him and beamed.

"Is everyone okay?"

Charity's joyful eyes dimmed. "Not Michael. He was standing guard."

Simon nodded slowly.

Charity watched Cyril as other Messengers welcomed him with happy embraces.

"And Spence?"

Simon looked down and shook his head. Charity sank, leaning her head on his shoulder. They studied the new entrance to the City, revealed to all.

"Where's Ella?"

Charity lifted her head and smiled.

"With Jack. All the officers fled when they called the retreat."

Simon laughed, eager to see his friend. Later.

"Looks like I'll have a good birthday after all," Charity mused.

"Looks like I'll have a birthday," Simon laughed.

"Do you think your grandma will keep looking for you?"

"I have no idea," Simon admitted. He ran a hand through his hair, leaving it disheveled; a few pieces fell in front of his eyes. "I hope she'll find more important things to do."

"What about your uncle?"

Simon thought back to the key in his cell door and the swift movement he sensed down the hallway. "I have a strange feeling we'll meet again. I can't believe I'm saying this, but I hope so."

Charity turned to look Simon straight in the eye. Her face was open, searching. She shook her head in disbelief and turned back to the City.

"Simon?" Charity asked. "This isn't over, is it?"

Simon pulled her close to his side and kissed her forehead. "No. It's only beginning."

Chapter Thirty

The Day will come, and I have seen a glimpse. Oh, to describe the beauty and majesty! My words fail me. Even if I could write all that Jesus had done on earth, the whole world could not contain the books. And to describe eternity? I can only share a fore-taste of what is to come.

Nations will join as one, giving glory to their Redeemer. "Holy, holy, holy, is the Lord God Almighty, who was and is and is to come!"

I will see my brother again. And my brothers. And my Brother. He will wipe away every tear from my eyes.

Amen. Come, Lord Jesus!

The grace of the Lord Jesus be with us all. Amen.

Acknowledgments

What do you say at the end of a series? This has been an adventure I never could have anticipated. Not only has God gifted me with friends in Simon, Charity, and Zeke, but He has also blessed me with countless friendships in all of you. Dear Messengers, thank you for the prayers, reviews, notes, encouragement, ideas, and enthusiasm. I'm overwhelmed by your love and support. Most of all, thank you for sharing the Message worth dying for.

There is no reason why I should be the one to have written these books, and yet God chose me to do so. I thank Him for all the ways He uses me to His glory. I continue to pray that He gives me what I need to do what He calls me to do, and I pray the same for you. More than anything, I thank our loving God for grace undeserved and life eternal.

Thank you, Matt, for your love for the Lord, for His people, and for me. Your constant encouragement kept me going with your urgent "people need these books!"

I'm grateful that I get to spend my life with you; you make it so much better. Thank you, Noah and Anna, for encouraging me and for being proud of me. It means so much. Thanks to you all for your patience as I read my rough draft to you, editing along the way.

Bruce, Jonathan, and Paul, thank you for your support and encouragement. Thank you for serving our youth by giving them the truth in a new way. Peggy Kuethe, I had no clue that my "hey, I have an idea" would result in your "this needs to happen." Thanks for advocating for Simon and all the Messengers. My team: Mark, Lisa, Lorraine, Cindy, Mary, and Pete. Thanks for being patient with me and for cheering me on. Pam, Joe, and Mark: thanks for your encouragement at just the right time. Readers, reviewers, and friends, there are too many to thank! But special thanks go to Laura, Heather, Colleen, Katie, Heidi, Rick, Jen, Melissa, Peter, Tim, Simeon, Macee, Faith, and so many others.

Loren, Holli, Cheryl, Elizabeth, Lindsey, Hannah, and Pam, thank you for your diligence in getting Simon out to those who need to meet him. Tim, Vicky, Mike, Sara, and Alex: thank you for making The Messengers look so much cooler than I am! Jamie and Emily, your precision and patience are priceless! Mark, Jeremy, Matt, and Bob: thank you so very much for hanging out in Spence's cellar. Ella thanks you for all the help with her car.

Rev. Dr. Wakseyoum Idosa and Rev. Yonas Yigezu, and the Ethiopian Evangelical Church Mekane Yesus, thank you for the permission to quote "When I Behold Jesus Christ" by Almaz Belhu. It is a blessing to share the Church's song around the world. I am honored to be your sister in Christ.

Bill, Karen, Jon, Gail, Tim, Heather: thank you for your love and support. Launch Teams: thank you for spreading the Message and making me laugh! Teachers, students, pastors, youth, parents, and leaders: I can't tell you what a joy it has been to be a part of your lives. Dear Ascension family: I love you all.

This book does not belong to me. Many hands labored to create, improve, share, and read it. We made this book together, with the help of God. To Him be the glory.

The λόγος remains.

Discussion Questions

The opening narrative introduces a new believer from the past. How does his struggle appear in the Church today? (Any guess who it could be?)

Simon and Jack are both struggling with identity. How are those struggles different?

Charity is changing; list some examples of how she is different from the teen Simon met in the Arena. What predictions do you have for her throughout this book?

Ella's Baptism is a wonderful moment, but it is tainted with conflict. List some of the conflicts shown. How do they relate to the opening narrative of chapter 1?

CHAPTER THREE

A nighttime visitor inspects the workshop. What are your reactions to this scene? Any predictions of who this character is? Any predictions of what will happen with this character throughout the novel?

Imagine that you live in New Morgan and your family was nothing but a memory. How would you describe your childhood to someone else?

CHAPTER FOUR

Describe the relationship between Jack and Simon. How has it changed over time? What has remained the same?

What was the biggest surprise for you during this chapter? What is your reaction to it?

CHAPTER FIVE

Consider the verse Jack read, Romans 8:18. How might it relate to the Messengers in New Morgan? How might it relate to you?

Discuss the relationship between Charity and Simon. What factors have brought them closer together? What factors had kept them apart?

CHAPTER SIX

"Let's face it, Simon. You aren't normal. You aren't supposed to be." Jack might be teasing, but there is truth to these words. In what ways is Simon "supposed to be" different? How does that apply to all believers?

Consider Chin's story. How does it relate to other Messengers in New Morgan? How does it relate to others you know or have heard about?

CHAPTER SEVEN

A common theme in these novels is when the Messengers encourage one another by reciting Bible passages. What is a favorite

Bible passage of yours? How do you use it in everyday life?

What predictions do you have for Malachi in this novel? What are your thoughts about Simon's interaction with Malachi lately?

CHAPTER EIGHT

It's now clear that the visitor is Roderick Druck Jr. How would you describe him? Has your impression of him changed since the first novel?

What does Simon think of Centra? What do you think of it?

CHAPTER NINE

Consider all the physical challenges Simon has endured over the past year. Can you make a list? How does this relate to some of the themes of this book?

Discuss the similarities and differences between Zeke and Glen.

CHAPTER TEN

Do you know who the person in the narrative is now? Consider the theme of brothers and sisters in Christ. How does this affect our lives together?

Simon is seeing a pattern, and Spence is a part of it. What does Simon realize about those who feel justified in hurting others?

CHAPTER ELEVEN

Charity had been given a label. How has she changed the symbol, as well as its meaning? Do we label others? Do others label us? Consider the lesson Charity has learned.

Simon takes interest in Psalm 142. Who wrote it? What kind of parallels might you make between Simon and the psalmist?

CHAPTER TWELVE

Think about Malachi. What role does he have among the Messengers?

The Messengers face a difficult challenge: mixed messages. Discuss parallels to your world today.

Chapter Thirteen

Consider Roderick and his relationship with his mother. How has it changed over the past year? What predictions do you have?

What does Simon learn about Malachi in this chapter? What are your reactions to their conversations?

Chapter Fourteen

Simon comes back to unhappy news. Was the mission worth it?

The chapter ends with Simon and Charity. How would you describe their relationship? How has Charity changed Simon? How has Simon changed Charity?

Chapter Fifteen

What roles does Ella have in the Messengers? Summarize the struggles she is enduring at the moment.

Jack and Simon have an important conversation about government. If you lived in New Morgan and were part of this conversation, what would you say?

Chapter Sixteen

Simon's access to the outside world has been severely limited. What kind of news has Ella been sharing about the world above? Which information has been most difficult, in your opinion?

What does Simon learn about Abby? How does this fit with what we knew of her before? What were surprises?

Chapter Seventeen

Simon and Jack talk about Jonathan. How many different ways did Jonathan serve the Messengers?

How does Simon serve Mrs. Meyer? How does Mrs. Meyer serve Simon?

Chapter Eighteen

"To his horror, she smiled back." What are the implications of this sentence? What does it say about Druck? about this girl? about New Morgan?

"Whether the trumpets sound or whether Jericho falls, we will see you again." Simon and his grandparents speak in code, using biblical imagery. What are Simon's grandparents trying to say here?

Chapter Nineteen

What are your thoughts on each member of the Pharen household?

Consider the life of John. What kinds of things did he live through?

Chapter Twenty

Charity, Simon, and Ella think of three plans. What do you predict will happen?

Spence and Cyril are still missing. How is that affecting the Messengers?

Chapter Twenty-One

Imagine you are a citizen who wakes up in the morning to find scattered propaganda on your doorstep. What would you think? What messages would you find?

"'One mission down,' she reported. 'Two more
to go.'" Charity ends the chapter with these
words. To adapt Jonathan's familiar words,
"Is it worth the trouble?"

Someone asks you to describe Zeke. What
would you say? Do you know someone like
him?

Think of a special school or building in your
life. Now, imagine it to be nothing but
rubble. What would it look like? How would
you feel if you saw it this way?

Describe Druck's primary goal. How has this
affected other aspects of his life?

Consider Simon's role as a Messenger. How have
relationships changed the way he makes
decisions?

"The details might be different, but he'd been in
enough prison cells to know what one felt
like." How do Simon's experiences reflect

the Early Church? How do they reflect the church today?

"Simon saw the look of horror on his uncle's face when he smiled." What other scene does this remind you of? What connections can you make?

CHAPTER TWENTY-FIVE

Consider Spence as a Messenger. How would you describe him to a friend?

Cyril says, "Someday, I will know peace. In that, I have great hope." How is he able to say this, even in his current condition?

CHAPTER TWENTY-SIX

Simon runs through the questions his father used to ask. How does he answer? How would you answer?

"Let's be honest, Uncle. You don't want my death. You want answers." Do you think Simon is right? If so, what kinds of answers does he want?

Chapter Twenty-Seven

Simon spends time talking with his uncle, and he is drained. How do you think the conversation went? Imagine a dialogue.

"Why waste your time on your enemies?" Druck asks. Consider how Druck sees the Messengers. In your experience, how do others view Christians?

Chapter Twenty-Eight

Druck leaves the door open again. Why? What predictions do you have for him in the years to come?

"A Bible? What would you need a Bible for?" How does Simon react to the soldier? How did you react?

Chapter Twenty-Nine

The facades of Westbend are crumbling. What is revealed?

Simon borrows his father's words to say that this is only the beginning. How so? What could happen next?

CHAPTER THIRTY

Over the past three books, we have heard from Mark, Peter, and John. How are their stories repeated in New Morgan? How are they repeated where you live?

Amen. Come, Lord Jesus! Do you ever pray this prayer?